SCREAMS OF THE SEASON

CRITTER CATCHERS
BOOK 5

HANK EDWARDS

MITTEN GINGER MEDIA

CONTENTS

SUMMARY

A Christmas spent far from home. Cody's father gone missing. Clues that point to another monster case.

Demetrius accompanies Cody on a trip to visit his parents in Colorado for Christmas. The house is packed with Cody's four brothers and their extended families, which is something close to chaos and means Cody and Demetrius are sleeping on the living room floor of Grant, his oldest brother. Soon after their arrival, they learn Cody's father's truck has been found in a ditch with no sign of his father and are out the door.

Everything going crazy around them makes Cody appreciate what he and Demmy have found together, and he opens up to his family about the true depth of their relationship. There are mixed reactions, but Cody's honesty with his family proves to Demetrius just how important he's become to Cody, and he realizes he couldn't ask for a better Christmas gift.

Between Greg Bower's disappearance, Grant's cannabis greenhouse, and a trip to the mall with Cody's nieces and nephews, the guys also manage to find themselves smack dab in the middle of another monster case when a Sasquatch makes a terrifying appearance. As they high-step for their lives through the deep Colorado snow, they'll end up saving a movie stuntman with a terrible sense of direction and writing Cody's nephew an IOU for a brand new drone.

Scream of the Season ©2018 Hank Edwards
Cover design by Adrian Nichols
Book design and production by Hank Edwards
Editing by Jerry Wheeler

First Publication, 2018

CHAPTER ONE

Demetrius was pretty sure he'd lost his mind.

He looked around the disaster in the kitchen and wondered what the hell he had been thinking. Every pot, pan, platter, serving bowl, plate, kitchen utensil, and dishtowel had been used. Granted, the whole house was filled with the savory aroma of cooking food, but he had really made a mess of Aunt Amelia's kitchen.

Correction: his and Cody's kitchen.

He wondered if he'd ever start thinking of the house as theirs instead of Amelia's, but he didn't have time to dwell on that. In a little over an hour, the house would be filled with people, and Demetrius was going to serve them his first attempt at a Thanksgiving meal.

There had to be at least a little insanity somewhere in his family tree.

He opened the oven and lifted the butter-soaked cheese-cloth to peek at the turkey. The skin was golden brown, but the button that indicated it was done had yet to pop. After a few squirts from the baster, he replaced the cheesecloth and closed the door. He looked at the mess all around him. It was difficult to keep his train of thought with such chaos. What was next? Mashed potatoes.

He turned up the burner under the pot of water just covering the peeled and quartered potatoes and stepped back. That would take some time to boil. Now what?

He tried not to think about how long cleaning up the mess would take. Through the doorway to the dining room, he noticed the table wasn't set, and he frowned.

"Cody?"

No reply. Demetrius walked through the dining room to the doorway that opened on the living room and leaned out. "CODY!"

"What?" he heard from somewhere down the hall. Demetrius hoped he wasn't lying on their bed watching TV.

"I need some help." He started back toward the kitchen, then turned to add, "Please!"

A short time later, Cody walked into the kitchen and stopped to stare. "Wow. You really messed this place up."

"Yeah, I know. Where have you been?"

"Cleaning the bathroom, just like you ordered." Cody held his fingers up in front of his mouth and widened his eyes. "Oops. I meant asked."

"Cute."

"Yeah, I am. But not as cute as you are in that sexy getup. Makes me want to baste you in my love juices."

"Love juices?"

Cody shrugged. "I was going for a sexy Thanksgiving kind of thing."

"Well, you didn't get there."

"You still look cute."

Demetrius looked down at his tank top, basketball shorts, and ankle-high white socks, all covered by a white apron splattered with food stains. The kitchen was small and heated up quick, so he had dressed light. "This outfit turns you on?"

Cody put his arms around him from behind and pulled Demetrius up against him. "Pretty much everything you wear turns me on." He kissed the side of Demetrius's neck, making him giggle.

"Stop that. We don't have time."

"Yeah, you're right. Because you invited half of Parson's Hollow to our first Thanksgiving together."

Demetrius sighed. He had no idea what he had been thinking. All he had wanted was to celebrate Thanksgiving as a couple in their new home with people they cared about. He had, of course, invited Aunt Amelia and Otis, her boyfriend she had moved in with. At the office a couple of days later, Demetrius learned Darnell "Jugs" Perramon's parents had moved to Florida, and Jugs was planning to split a turkey pot pie with his adopted Yorkie Enid Helen, so Demetrius had invited him to dinner. From there the list had expanded to include Demetrius's ex-boyfriend Oliver along with his new boyfriend, Wick, and Oliver's grandmother, Eileen, as well as Lucia Durant and Zenona Baldwin, two of Cody's ex-girlfriends who had helped Cody announce his feelings for Demetrius to the rest of the town.

He couldn't do this. It was all going to fall apart, and their guests would find him curled into a ball in a corner of the kitchen, sobbing.

"You in there?"

Cody's voice brought him out of his thoughts.

"Yeah, I'm here. Just remind me of how stressful this is when Christmas rolls around, and I get the idea to do it all over again."

"You've got a deal." Cody slid his hands beneath the apron and down the front of Demetrius's shorts. "Do you need to relax?"

Demetrius closed his eyes as he leaned back against Cody. "I really do. But I don't have time. Will you get the tablecloth out of the bottom drawer of the buffet and set the table?"

Cody kissed his neck before removing his hands. "Spoilsport."

"We'll have fun later," Demetrius said. "I promise."

"I'll hold you to that."

Demetrius put together the green bean casserole as Cody set the dining room table. The clatter and clink of the dishes and silverware helped him relax, and he felt much better by the time he slid the casserole into the oven alongside the turkey. The potatoes were boiling and just about ready to mash, and the turkey still looked good.

Maybe they would be able to pull this off after all.

"What do you think?" Cody asked.

Demetrius walked to the dining room doorway and smiled. The white linen tablecloth he had picked up at Harker's Home Goods fit Amelia's dining table perfectly, and the forest green placemats helped the white place settings his parents had given him stand out.

Cody looked at him from the other end of the table.

"I guess this is it, huh?" Cody said.

"This is what?"

"We're hosting a Thanksgiving dinner party. We're officially a couple. There's no going back now."

Demetrius grinned and walked around the table to pull him into a hug.

"You feeling a little scared about all of this, big guy?" Demetrius whispered as he held Cody tight.

Cody pulled back and smiled down at him. "Not in the least. I just hope you don't want to make a run for it."

"It's going to take more than a house filled with our friends and family to scare me off." The oven timer buzzed and Demetrius smiled. "And our guests are going to be here in less than an hour. Go get your shower while I finish up in the kitchen."

"You don't need my help?"

"I know how you are around food. You'll end up sneaking more than we'll serve," Demetrius said as he walked into the kitchen and turned off the buzzer.

Cody followed him. "You know me too well."

"That I do."

Demetrius put on the oven mitts. Before he could open the oven door to reach in for the turkey, Cody took him by the shoulders and turned him around. "Hey."

"What?"

Cody gave him a soft kiss. No tongue, no groping, just a sweet, gentle kiss, and the feel of it sent shivers through Demetrius.

"I'm glad you wanted to do this," Cody said.

"Even with Oliver and Lucia and Zenona coming?"

Cody nodded. "And Jugs and Eileen and Ollie's boyfriend Wank."

"Oliver doesn't like when you call him Ollie. And his boyfriend's name is Wick."

"Right, Wick. I'm sure I won't mess that up. Who names their kid Wick? But seriously, I know today has been crazy and you've been working your ass off, and we're probably deep in debt from buying all of this food. But this just feels right. You know?"

"It does." Demetrius stood on his toes to kiss Cody once more. Still wearing the oven mitts, he squeezed his crotch. "Now go get showered."

"That oven mitt felt pretty damn good. We might need to bring those into the bedroom later."

"Go."

Cody walked away, chuckling. Demetrius watched him

go, and then he pulled the turkey out of the oven. The button had popped. So far, so good.

JUGS WAS FIRST TO ARRIVE. He carried Enid Helen in the crook of one arm and a pan of fresh baked cornbread in the other. Enid Helen trotted all around the house, sniffing and yipping, her claws tip-tapping on the kitchen linoleum as she begged for scraps. Cody handed Jugs a beer and told him to sit down and watch the football game.

Lucia and Zenona arrived together. Lucia brought candied yams covered with marshmallows, and Zenona a bowl of homemade cranberry relish.

"Glad to see you haven't burned the place down yet," Lucia said once Cody handed her a beer.

"I think Amelia would skin us both if that happened." He looked at Zenona. "Beer?"

"Have any wine?" Zenona asked. "Chardonnay?"

"Ollie and Eileen are bringing the wine. I can give you a beer for now or a ginger ale or glass of filtered water."

"Water's fine."

"Ollie? Is he talking about your ex, Oliver Berridge?" Lucia asked Demetrius.

"That's right. He lives with his grandmother in Pinesville, New Jersey now."

"And you're okay with him being here today?" she said to Cody.

"He's coming with his grandmother, who's hilarious, and his new boyfriend, Wank."

"Wick," Demetrius corrected, trying to focus on the gravy recipe displayed on a web page on his phone.

"Right, that's what I said."

Zenona stepped up beside Demetrius. "Need help? I'm a gravy whisperer."

Demetrius gave her a big, relieved smile. "Yes, please. I found a recipe online, but I've lost my place twice now trying to read it."

"Mash the potatoes, I've got this."

"You're amazing. Thank you."

Amelia and her boyfriend Otis arrived with two pies, one pumpkin and the other pecan. Shortly after that, Oliver, Wick, and Eileen rang the bell and Cody let them in. Wick was cute and blond and seemed friendly but nervous. Demetrius was glad they didn't look anything alike, otherwise Cody would have never let him live it down. Everyone was introduced and tossed their coats on the bed. Jugs scooped up Enid Helen to keep her from being stepped on. Cody opened the bottles of wine and filled glasses as everyone found a seat at the table. Demetrius was happy to see they all fit, with enough elbow room to allow them to eat comfortably.

Once the turkey was carved and all the side dishes placed on the table, Demetrius and Cody sat at opposite ends of the table and smiled at each other.

"You two are so damn cute," Amelia said, lifting her wine glass. "To Demetrius and Cody. Thank you for having us all here today."

Everyone raised a glass, and Demetrius took a deep drink of his pinot noir as the countless tiny knots of tension in his belly started to loosen.

"Before we begin, I think we should all say what we're thankful for," Lucia said. "I'm thankful Demetrius invited me here today. And even though Cody has dated every girl in town and he often irritates my very soul, I'm thankful he finally found someone who keeps his interest. Not to mention that he helped a group of us who may never have met become friends."

"You're welcome?" Cody said, cocking his head and frowning as he looked at Demetrius.

Zenona was thankful for her friends and that her family was healthy back in Italy. Amelia was thankful for her family and Otis, and Otis was thankful for Viagra. Jugs was thankful for finding Enid Helen, who sat patiently by his chair, as well as his job at Critter Catchers. Oliver thanked Demetrius and Cody for hosting dinner and inviting them, and Eileen was thankful she'd had an adventure with them two months prior back home in Pinesville. Wick was thankful he'd met Oliver, and Demetrius thanked Amelia for letting them live in her house and keep her dining room table with both expansion leaves. Cody gave thanks he had managed to bring home a Critter Catchers paycheck earlier that month and for how full he would feel later.

With the thanks out of the way, they all dug in. The turkey was juicy and delicious, the mashed potatoes smooth and fluffy, and Zenona's gravy was the perfect complement. The stuffing was moist and well-seasoned, and the green bean casserole the right consistency. Lucia's candied yams gave Demetrius a sugar buzz, and Zenona's cranberry relish had a citrusy zing.

Conversation and laughter accompanied the scrape of silverware and serving utensils. By the time everyone had eaten their fill, most of them looked comatose. They decided as a group to take a break before pie, and each person groaned upon standing up. Some staggered into the living room to watch the end of the football game, and the rest helped clear the table and dole out leftovers.

Cody had bought several sets of cheap reusable containers, so he set aside a good portion of food for guests to take home. Lucia and Zenona divided up the food and wrote names on the containers as Demetrius started washing dishes.

Amelia stood beside him with a dishtowel, drying each dish as he finished rinsing and putting it away.

"You put everything in the same place I had it," Amelia said as she stacked the plates. "Makes this so much easier."

"You had the kitchen well-organized. Why would I change that?" Demetrius surveyed the roaster and pots stacked in rows waiting on the stovetop. "But we are definitely going to look into installing a dishwasher."

"That was on my list of things to do, but…" She shrugged as she grinned.

"You found a good man to move in with instead," Demetrius finished for her, and they both laughed.

"And so did you."

"I guess we both lucked out, didn't we?"

Amelia squeezed his shoulder. "We surely did. Now pull off those gloves and let's join your guests. Sounds like things are getting rowdy in the other room."

A few hours later, only Eileen, Oliver and Wick remained. They helped with last minute tidying up and putting away the last of the dishes as Cody finished washing the pots and roaster. Wick handed Demetrius the wine glasses, and he put them on the shelf of the dining room buffet.

"These are nice glasses," Wick said.

Demetrius dropped his voice to a loud whisper. "I got them at Target for half price."

"I love those kinds of finds." Wick smiled, showing off a set of deep dimples. He was cute in a preppy sort of way, with his blond hair parted on the left side, and a trim goatee and mustache.

"How long have you and Oliver been dating?"

"About three weeks. My parents are divorced and both live out of state, so it was nice of you to include me in the invitation."

"No one should be alone on Thanksgiving." Demetrius put

the last wine glass away and yawned when he stood up. "Sorry. It's been a long day."

Oliver walked out of the kitchen with Eileen, and shared a smile with Wick. The sight made Demetrius feel good. He liked Oliver as a friend and was glad he'd found someone.

"All right, lovebirds," Eileen said in her raspy, cigarette-honed voice. "Let's hit the road."

"You're not driving back tonight?" Demetrius said.

"We have a couple of rooms out at the Westbrooke Motor Lodge," Oliver said.

Cody leaned in the kitchen doorway, drying his hands. "That place is all class."

Oliver looked at him with raised eyebrows. "Been there often?"

"All right, Ollie," Cody said, throwing a glance toward Demetrius. "Don't ruin a fine day by turning your sass up to eleven."

"Does it ever go below eleven?" Wick asked.

Everyone laughed, and Cody dropped a hand on Wick's shoulder. "I like your new man, Ollie."

"Now that you know my name?" Wick grinned.

"I only slipped up once."

"Twice."

"What did he call you?" Oliver asked.

"Wank."

"Cody…" Demetrius said.

"What? I'm sure it's happened to him often. Right?"

Wick shook his head. "Not at all, actually."

"Well, there you go. Now you and Ollie have something to tell your grandkids."

Eileen let out a laugh that sounded like a rusty buzz saw. "I can't wait to be a great-grandmother." She stepped between Oliver and Wick and put her arms around their shoulders. "You boys going to try for a baby tonight?"

"Oh my god, Grandma." Oliver's blush was so deep, Demetrius thought it might have covered his whole body.

"Well, you better get to it." Cody gave them their leftovers. "Rooms at the Westbrooke all have kitchenettes, so you can store these in the fridge and even heat them up in the microwave after you work up an appetite."

Eileen laughed as Wick took the bags from Cody. She held out her arms and Cody leaned down to give her a strong hug.

"I like you, Cody. I wish you lived closer to Pinesville."

"I like you, too, Eileen. And if you ever move closer to Parson's Hollow, give me a call."

Demetrius hugged Oliver, then Eileen, and awkwardly did the same for Wick as he held the bags of food. He walked to the door with them and they all exclaimed at the fat snowflakes steadily falling. Oliver and Wick each carried a bag of leftovers and put Eileen between them, her arms linked with each of theirs as they went down the front steps and across the lawn to Oliver's car. With a final wave as they drove off, Demetrius shut and locked the door, then leaned back against it. He closed his eyes and blew out a long, slow breath.

"Look what I found."

Demetrius opened his eyes. Cody held two wine glasses filled almost to the brim with red wine.

"There's wine left?"

"Not any more."

"I really need this." Demetrius accepted one of the glasses and smiled when Cody kissed him.

"Happy Thanksgiving," Cody whispered, kissing him again.

"Happy Thanksgiving."

"Want to stretch out on the couch with your hot man?"

"Yeah." Demetrius walked down the hall, speaking over his shoulder. "When he gets here, tell him I'll be right out."

"That's not funny," Cody called after him. "Kind of hurtful, actually."

"I need to get out of these jeans. I can barely breathe."

Cody was at the bedroom door moments later, his own pants and briefs around his ankles. His cock was at half-mast as he fumbled with his shirt buttons. "I thought our guests would never leave, too."

"Whoa there, cowboy. I'm way too full of turkey and starchy side dishes to even think about sex."

"Yeah, I knew that." Cody kicked aside his pants and briefs and peeled off his shirt, standing before Demetrius in just his socks. "I was making sure you weren't interested in some after dinner carnality, that's all."

"Carnality?"

"It's a word." He opened a dresser drawer and pulled out a pair of house pants. "Look it up."

"Let's just change and sit down."

Demetrius felt much better once he wore pants with an elastic waistband. He returned to the living room to find Cody stretched out on the couch watching a Christmas movie.

"Got room for me?"

Cody smiled and opened up his arms. "Come aboard."

Demetrius lay alongside him and sighed when Cody wrapped his arms around him. He was full, slightly drunk on wine, and lying with his best friend and lover. What more could he want?

Cody's phone buzzed on the coffee table.

"I'm too comfortable," Cody muttered in Demetrius's ear.

"Could be important. All of our guests just left, and it's snowing out."

"All of those guests would call your phone instead of mine."

"Not Jugs. Or Zenona and Lucia."

"Fine." Cody shifted position and looked at the display. "It's my Mom."

"Aw, she wants to wish you a happy Thanksgiving."

"Yeah."

The phone buzzed again.

"You'll have to talk to her later if you don't answer it now."

"I know."

"I'll keep quiet."

"It's not that. Well, not all that. I'm just really full, too."

The phone stopped buzzing.

"So, call her back in a little while." Demetrius yawned and reached for his wine glass, surprised to discover it was nearly empty. When had that happened?

"It's nice just laying here with you," Cody said, and he yawned as well.

"I think everyone enjoyed dinner, don't you?"

"Absolutely. Looked like even Lucia had a good time."

"She and Zenona have become good friends, it seems," Demetrius said.

"Maybe being one of my ex-girlfriends can be seen as a good thing."

"I don't know if I'd go that far."

Cody's phone buzzed once, and he lifted it to look at the display. "Text message. From Mom."

"Everything okay?"

"Well, that would depend on your definition of okay."

"What's that mean?"

"She wants me to fly out there for Christmas."

CHAPTER TWO

Cody handed the live trap down the folding attic steps to Demmy. The squirrel inside darted from one end of the trap to the other, claws scrabbling across the metal.

"How many more are up there?" Demmy asked.

"Three more cages."

"That's a lot of squirrels."

"It's kind of nutty."

Demmy shook his head. "Boo. Bad joke."

"Look, cut me some slack. I'm still full from yesterday."

"You ate an entire plate of leftovers for breakfast this morning."

"Which was what we had for dinner yesterday. Therefore, I'm still full from yesterday."

"You're impossible."

"Which is why you like me."

"Less talking and more squirrel transferring, please."

When they had all four squirrels in the back of the truck, Cody went over the invoice with the customer and accepted a check from her.

"I'm so glad you got them all out of the house." By Cody's

estimate, the woman was in her early forties and wore her lipstick a little thick. "I heard them running around up there, and it just put my nerves on end."

"This time of year, they're looking for a place to hole up for the winter."

She smiled and twirled a lock of hair around her finger. "Aren't we all?"

Cody smiled. "Yes, indeed. You have a good day now, Mrs. Bomeister."

"Ms. Bomeister."

He smiled again and quickly walked down the porch steps to get in the passenger seat of Demmy's truck.

"Full amount? No discount?" Demmy asked.

"Full amount. And I dodged what felt like a come on."

"Really?" Demmy looked at Ms. Bomeister standing on the porch watching them drive off. "She was nice. And pretty."

Cody put his hand on Demmy's thigh and squeezed. "Not as pretty as you. And you don't wear as much lipstick."

"What a relief." He drove in silence for a time. "Did you call or text your Mom yet?"

Cody looked out his window and shook his head. "Not yet."

"Just call her. How long has it been since you've seen your parents?"

"Five years."

"That's much too long."

"Yeah, but she wants me out there for Christmas."

"Right. That's when families usually get together."

Cody looked at Demmy's profile. He loved the sight, no matter if they were in the truck, at work, or in bed. Even though he'd seen Demmy's profile for the majority of his life, he never thought he'd get tired of it.

"What would you do for Christmas?"

"Oh." Demmy glanced at him. "I didn't think about it like that. I'll be with Amelia and Otis, so I won't be alone."

"I know that. But I don't want to be away from you. It's our first Christmas as a couple. I want to spend it together, the two of us."

"Oh. Oh wow." Tears shone in Demmy's eyes. "That's probably the most amazing thing anyone has ever said to me."

"Pull over."

"What? But there's nowhere to pull off."

"Just pull onto the shoulder."

Demmy eased the truck over. Cody released his seatbelt and leaned over the console. Taking Demmy's face in his hands, he gently turned his head. Demmy's blue eyes were filled with tears, and one ran down his cheek.

"I'm not just having fun with you." Cody could hear the hitch in his own voice. "I really want to make sure you understand I get how important this is between us."

Demmy nodded between Cody's palms. "I know you're all in. I do."

"Good. Because I really don't want to be apart for the holidays." He kissed him, still holding his face between both hands. "If I go to Colorado to see my parents, I want you to go, too."

A smile now. "You do? All right. Yeah."

Cody smiled back and kissed him again. He lingered this time, tracing Demmy's lips with his tongue. A couple of cars sped past, but he couldn't care less. He needed to savor this moment.

The squirrels scampered about in the cages, one of them making a screeching sound that pretty much ruined the mood. Cody pulled back, and they shared a smile.

"Homophobic squirrel?" Demmy said.

"He must avoid nuts."

"Bad joke."

"You're welcome." Cody moved back into his seat. "You sure about going with me for Christmas? From what my mom said in her voice mail, the whole family will be there."

"A Bower family Christmas? How could I resist?"

"You say that like it's a good thing."

"Your family is a lot to handle." Demmy checked for traffic before pulling onto the road. "But that's kind of the fun of it."

"When you can leave the house and get away from them, yeah, they're fun. But not when you're staying right smack dab in the middle with nowhere to run."

"Sounds like you're having second thoughts about going." Demmy glanced at him. "Anything else going on?"

"Nothing specific. I would like to see my folks and a brother or two. Just not all of them, really."

"You're talking about Roman."

"Yeah."

"When was the last time you talked with him?"

"Hell, I don't know. He's not really the type of guy who calls to check in, you know?"

"You could call him, you know."

Cody groaned. "We don't have anything in common. He's wound so tight, it's nearly impossible to talk with him about anything. There's no conversation with Roman. It's all statements and judgment."

They'd reached Gullet Trail and Demmy turned onto the dirt road. Gullet Trail meandered through Parson's Wood for several miles, snaking a circuitous route around Parson's Pond. The sun sparkled on the water as the trail climbed the hills around the pond.

"You know for sure Roman's going to be there?"

"Seems that way. Roman and his beautiful, cold, and perfect wife, Madison, and their two perfect kids, Summer and Brock."

"I thought Brock was the name of one of Grant's kids?"

"No, that's Brooke, Grant's daughter with his girlfriend Mac."

"Oh, that's right."

Demmy pulled off the trail in their usual spot and they got out. They'd released the majority of the critters they'd caught here. In minutes, the four squirrels had scrambled up trees, and the empty cages were in the back of the truck. When Demmy reached for the keys, Cody touched his arm.

"Do we have to leave right away?"

"No. We don't have another appointment today." Demmy leaned forward to look up at the trees. "You worried about the squirrels?"

"No. I just thought it was a nice day, and we could maybe, you know."

Demmy grinned. "Oh yeah?" He checked the trail behind them in the mirrors. "You don't think we'll get caught?"

"Hell, half of this town was conceived out here around Parson's Pond. Come on, we need to work off that big meal yesterday."

"How do you suggest we do this? There's a big console between us."

"There's some room in the back."

"I don't think we can both fit back there."

"Won't know until we try."

They got out and moved both front seats up as far as possible. That left more room than Cody had anticipated, and he got into the back and stretched out along the narrow bench seat. Demmy climbed in from the driver's side and reached back to close the door. He moved carefully, putting one knee between Cody's legs and leaning forward to kiss him. Cody curled his tongue around Demmy's as he slid his hands up and down his back. Cool air drifted in from the windows they'd left open a couple of inches, and Cody could hear squirrels chattering. He wondered if they were the ones they'd released, then decided he didn't care when Demmy moved down to his neck.

"Oh, you know that spot," Cody said, sliding both hands down over Demmy's ass and squeezing.

Demmy unbuttoned Cody's shirt and spread it wide, and then he ran his tongue along his torso to the top of his jeans. As Demmy circled his navel with his tongue, he opened Cody's jeans and reached inside to grab him tight.

Cody gasped. "Fuck, your hands are cold."

"Sorry."

"S'all right. Kind of a turn on, actually."

"I'll remember that."

Demmy pulled Cody's briefs down until the elastic waistband was beneath his balls, and then he sucked his cock, pumping up and down with his mouth. Cody moaned, one hand behind his head and the other on the back of Demmy's.

"Get up here," Cody said, surprised at the deep lust he heard in his own voice. "I want to suck you."

Demmy sucked the head of Cody's cock hard before releasing it with a loud pop that made the muscles in Cody's belly tremble. Demmy moved up until his cock was pointing right in his face, and Cody opened up to take him in, pinching Demmy's nipples as he sucked him.

"God, you're so good at that," Demmy whispered. "I love watching you suck me."

A sudden cramp in his neck forced Cody to stop. "Ow, cramp."

"Show me," Demmy said, rubbing the spot indicated until the muscle released.

"I really need to come, but we are pretty crowded in here," Cody said.

"I have an idea."

Demmy moved down until his cock lay on top of Cody's.

He held up a hand and let a long runner of spit drop onto his palm.

"I want both of our spit on us," Demmy said, holding his palm under Cody's mouth. "Spit."

Cody spat, and Demmy smeared it over both of their cocks. He held both of them in one hand and stroked, slowly at first until his fingers found the right position, then faster and faster.

"Just think about your big cock in my ass," Demmy said. "How hot and tight it feels as you fuck me."

"Goddamn, you're getting really fucking good at dirty talk," Cody said as he stared into Demmy's face. "And I'm going to fuck the hell out of you when we get home tonight."

"You going to be balls deep inside me?" Demmy said.

"Fuck, yeah. And I'm going to come so hard while I'm in there."

"Oh, fuck. I'm close."

"Me too. Don't stop."

Moments later, Cody grunted as he came, feeling the hot splash of it up his chest. Demmy kept hold of them both, his strokes fast as he leaned back, eyes closed tight and mouth open. Cody worked Demmy's nipples as he watched him, amazed at how much he had learned about his best friend the last few months.

"I'm coming," Demmy said with a gasp. "Oh, yeah."

Demmy came on Cody's chest and belly, and when he'd finished, he leaned down to give Cody a gentle kiss.

"So hot," Demmy whispered.

"You've got that right," Cody whispered back.

Something hit the hood of the truck with a loud bang, making them both jump. Demmy slid back as Cody sat up, both turning their heads to look out the windows.

"What the fuck was that?" Cody lifted his hips and pulled

up his jeans, grimacing at the sticky mess as he buttoned them.

"Something hit the truck."

"Yeah, but what?"

They ducked their heads at the bang on the roof of the truck right over them.

"Is someone throwing rocks at us?" Demmy looked around, his eyes wide. "Did they see us having sex?"

"Let's find out."

Cody pushed the passenger door open, walking quickly to the back of the truck, his shirt still unbuttoned. The cool air made the cum on his skin feel like ice.

"Who the fuck is out here?"

No answer but the wind and the talkative squirrels.

Another bang on the hood of the truck brought him whirling around on his heel. He didn't see anyone, but he had turned in time to see an acorn roll off the hood. The chattering and scrabble of claws drew his attention, and he looked up to see a couple of squirrels dash along a tree limb overhead.

"What's going on?" Demmy stood beside him, trying to get his clothes back in some kind of order.

"We're being bombed by the squirrels we evicted."

"You're kidding."

An acorn landed a few inches in front of them and they both looked up.

"They are really bitter," Demmy said.

"And their aim is improving."

"We should go."

As Demmy turned away, Cody grabbed his hand.

"If I go to Colorado to see my family over Christmas, you promise to go with me?"

Demmy moved closer, sliding his hands inside Cody's unbuttoned shirt and around to his back. He kissed a patch of skin scaly with their cum, took the hard nub of a nipple between his teeth for a moment, then stood on his toes to kiss him on the lips.

"I promise I will go to Colorado with you."

Another acorn banged off the roof.

"Let's get out of here before those rodents trash my truck," Demmy said.

Cody kissed him once more before they got inside and Demmy backed out from beneath the trees.

CHAPTER THREE

The heat and humidity inside the greenhouse provided a strange contrast to the thigh-deep Colorado snow outside. In the small entryway, Demetrius shed his coat, scarf, gloves, and hat, stuffing everything into one of the cubbies against the wall. He took off his boots, sitting in a nearby chair to pull on rubber-soled slip-on shoes.

"I like to keep everything as clean as possible. That's why outerwear is either removed or covered."

Demetrius looked up at Grant, the oldest of Alice Bower's five sons, and took the white, light-weight cotton coverall he'd extended to him. Grant exuded a laid back, almost sleepy aura, and his long dark hair hung in two braids, one over each shoulder. Demetrius had never really gotten to know Grant very well because he was seven years older than him and Cody. When he saw him on holidays and around the Bower home on occasion, he'd always seemed nice.

Demetrius smiled at Cody as he stepped into the coveralls. "We should have brought our own coveralls."

"Damn airline probably would have charged us extra for them," Cody grumbled as he tugged off a boot. He shot Grant an irritated look. "You go through this every fucking time you come in here?"

"Every time, little bro. Gotta keep the bad juju out of my crop."

"No wonder you're stoned all the time."

"Correct yourself. I'm not stoned all the time, just a good portion of the time. And it's all perfectly legal."

"How many plants do you have?" Demetrius asked.

"Twelve. It's the limit for personal use growers, and I'm not licensed to distribute to sellers. Lots of rules and regulations to follow for it all, you know? That lock on the outside of the door is required because no one under twenty-one is allowed inside. The kiddos have to stay skedaddled. To keep this place running, I've gotta stay focused and engaged."

Cody zipped up the coverall. "Okay, Captain Cannabis, we're all covered up."

Grant tousled his hair. "Not all of you."

Demetrius hid a smirk behind his hand as Cody glared.

"You're going to make me wear a hairnet?" Cody said.

Grant handed them each a hairnet. "It's part of the hygiene protocol."

"This is your personal greenhouse," Cody said, his voice almost a growl. "This is just a legal version of the setup you had in college, and that was in a dank closet with a grow light."

Grant sighed and grinned. "That dorm room was the best, man." He looked their hair over with a critical eye. "All right. No hairnets. But if I find a hair on one of my buds later, we're going to have a serious talk."

"I would prefer that conversation over this one," Cody said, and tossed the hairnet back at Grant. "Let's go."

"Right this way."

Demetrius nudged Cody as they followed Grant down a

short, narrow hallway. "Take it easy on him. None of this is his fault."

"Not his fault?" Cody whispered, stopping to let Grant get a little farther ahead. "It's all of their fault. Why didn't they tell me they'd built Grant his own pot greenhouse? Why wasn't I made aware of that fact?"

"Dudes?" Grant stood at a door with a marijuana leaf painted on it. "You okay back there?"

"We're fine, Willie Nelson, don't worry," Cody said.

Demetrius followed Cody up to the door, relieved to see Grant smiling.

"That is not the first time I've been compared to Willie Nelson." He waggled his braids at them. "And I promise you, it won't be the last."

"Your braids are really, um, even," Demetrius said. "You must have a lot of practice."

"Mac does the braids for me. I can pull it all back into a killer ponytail, but Mac's the braiding queen. Sometimes me and the kids all just sit in kitchen chairs in the apartment, and she rolls a desk chair from one of us to the next, braiding our hair. All four of us look awesome."

"Who braids Mac's hair?" Demetrius asked.

"Oh, she doesn't have hair. She shaves her head." Grant smiled before he opened the door and stepped into the greenhouse.

Cody waved for Demetrius to go first and he followed Grant, stopping just inside the door. The air inside the greenhouse was a lot more humid. It made him think of Parson's Hollow at the end of September, when they usually got a week or so of hot weather just before autumn rolled in. A few glass panels let in natural light, and he wondered how Grant kept the windows from fogging up. On a table that ran the length of the narrow space stood large ceramic pots, each with its own tall cannabis plant.

"Wow," Demetrius said.

"Pretty awesome, isn't it?" Grant smiled as he looked around. "I never get tired of stepping through the door."

"Oh my God," Cody said.

Demetrius thought Cody might pass out. He looked from the plants to Demetrius to Grant and back to the plants.

"Mom and Dad are growing pot," Cody said as he looked over the greenery. "A dozen pot plants."

"Mom and Dad are pretty cool, Codes."

"Don't call me that."

Grant shrugged. "Whatevs." He smiled at Demetrius. "Want to take a closer look, Dems?"

"Don't call him that."

"Dude, what is this harshness all about? Why are you so put-upon?"

"You want to know what's got me all riled up? Do you?"

"Cody…" Demetrius said in a low voice.

But Cody ignored him. He took a step closer to Grant and poked him in the chest a few times as he spouted off.

"I'm riled up for many reasons. First of all, no one picked us up at the airport, and we had to pay a fucking Uber driver almost a hundred dollars to cart our asses all the way out here. Mom knew when our plane was landing, and she told us someone would be there to meet us. But we stood outside baggage claim for forty minutes until she finally managed to text me back. And you know what she said? 'Oh, you're coming in today?' My own damn mother! Second, even with all the phone calls and emails and goddamn birthday and Christmas cards over the last few years, none of you felt the urge to share with me the fact that Mom and Dad invested a chunk of their retirement savings, our inheritance, into a greenhouse for you to grow pot. Or, to put it another way, Alice Bower, our mother, is growing pot. This is the same woman who once grounded me for two weeks when I was in high school because she found a beer can in the kitchen trash and suspected I had been drinking. She saw it in a trash can and just assumed it was mine, even though you and Roman were both around and old enough to drink. So that same woman has now gotten it into her head to let you grow a dozen pot plants in the backyard of her house!"

"I paid for half of the greenhouse," Grant corrected with a smile. "So they didn't pay for all of it. And Moms and Pops have been known to indulge in a taste of the green essence now and then as well."

The vein in Cody's temple throbbed as his eyes went wide. "What?"

Grant grinned. "Yeah, man. Pops has become really fond of Great Tokey Mountain, says it helps him sleep."

"Aren't the Great Smokey Mountains in Tennessee?" Demetrius asked.

"All one big planet, Dems. It's a great name, isn't it?"

"Yep, it's the best. Just had to ask, because it seems like it might be confusing. You know, to those who partake."

"All good, Dems, all good. Anyway, Moms and Pops are totes on board with all of this and are hip to the benefits. And I'm hoping to get a business license one day. But that's, like, a million more hoops to jump through, so I thought I'd start out small and learn a few things first."

Cody pressed his lips tight together, and he clenched his fists. Demetrius took a step closer, muscles tensed, ready to jump between them if Cody started swinging. They had been in Colorado all of three hours, and Cody's blood pressure was already dangerously high.

And there were three more days until Christmas.

"You're not helping me relax and feel better about this trip," Cody said.

Grant gestured toward a plant. "I've got something that could help."

Cody lifted a hand, palm out. "No. Thank you. I'll be fine. But I'm not really sure what you meant by wanting a business license. Could you enlighten me?"

"Us," Grant said.

"What?"

"You said I should enlighten you, but you should have said I should enlighten you plural." He gestured between Demetrius and Cody. "So, instead of 'Could you enlighten me,' you should have said, 'Could you enlighten us.' That way you're including Dems in the conversation." He smiled at Demetrius. "I wanted to make sure you didn't feel left out."

Demetrius gave a small wave as Cody started taking deep, gulping breaths. "Not a bit. I feel quite included, actually." He placed a hand on Cody's forearm, hoping his touch would help him calm down.

"Good. I know you must feel excluded from a lot of societal things, what with being gay and all. Though you can now get married and, in most states, I think, adopt children. So, that's pretty cool."

"Um, yeah. It is incredibly cool that all exists now. But, you were going to tell Cody and me about your plans for the, um, the greenhouse."

"We call it Hemp Hothouse."

Demetrius smiled. "Very creative. And can you tell us more about what you're trying to accomplish here in Hemp Hothouse? Other than the obvious: growing pot and getting stoned."

"I see myself as a product manager, you know? I assess the varieties of plants and buds and try new ones based on what affects they have. I've even started cross-pollinating plants, and created a new variety. And I'm a member of the local Seed Share community, too." He grinned and puffed out his chest. "I'm the Inventory Master."

"Impressive," Demetrius said. "And the Seed Share is

where you take the seeds collected from your plants and exchange them with other growers in the area?"

Grant's eyes widened, and he looked at Cody, whose face was a little less red than it had been just moments before. "Dems knows a lot about the business. Do you guys grow pot back in Parson's Hollow? Because how cool would that be if you did?"

Cody unclenched his jaw and said, "No, we don't grow pot back home, because back home, it's illegal. Can you understand that?"

"Codes, I'm completely zoomed in on what you're saying. You feel excluded and shunned by the core family, and I honor your right of ownership for those feelings. Mom's been working hard to get everything ready for Christmas, what with all of us coming together for the first time in years, and she forgot you guys were arriving today. I was busy out here trimming buds and talking to my big, leafy wonders. They do really well when I verbally encourage them to grow big buds. Sometimes I sing "I Like Big Butts," you know that song by Sir Mix-a-lot? Only I sing that I like big buds. They seem to really respond to that." Grant smiled, then looked Cody over. "Christmas stresses out a lot of people. It's one of the biggest selling times for pot out here, you know."

"I can't imagine why."

Cody crossed his arms and huffed, but Demetrius was glad to see him drop his shoulders down a bit. Maybe the outburst was just what he needed to get the frustration out of his system and allow them to focus on enjoying the holiday.

"And where the fuck are Mom and Dad? I've seen you, but where are they?"

Then again, he might need just a little bit longer.

As Grant absorbed more of Cody's frustrated tirade, Demetrius walked around the long table. The plants were big and beautiful, their leaves speckled with droplets of water due to what Demetrius assumed was a recent watering. Printed labels identified each variety of plant, and he smiled at some of the names: High Altitude, Granite Brainstorm, and Firestorm Free-for-all. Toward the end of the row, Demetrius found two plants with large buds, and he leaned in for a closer look. Some of the buds were huge, and extended a couple of feet above the plant.

Demetrius had smoked a few times in college but had never made a habit of it. It was illegal, for one, and the good stuff was expensive. He had gotten some skunky smelling pot the last time he'd sampled it, and the experience had put him off it since. But this stuff Grant was growing looked and smelled good. Maybe it was time to try again. And out here, it was legal.

He wondered if Cody's stress might benefit from a hit or twelve off some Great Tokey Mountain, High Altitude, or Granite Brainstorm.

Cody approached, and from his expression he was still miffed at his family.

"You doing okay?" Demetrius asked.

"Yeah. Fine. Whatever." He noticed the tall buds on the plant. "Holy shit, what the hell is going on with that plant? Look at the size of that bud."

Grant had walked up in time to hear Cody, and he said, "That's Carlos. He's one of my best producers of a new variety called Granite Brainstorm. I found the seeds for him at a seed exchange in Reno and started him about a year ago."

"Granite Brainstorm," Demetrius said. "That pretty much says it all, doesn't it?"

"For sure, man."

Grant's phone rang and he looked at the display. "Oh, this is Fleck, from the Seed Share group. I gotta take this. Look around, but don't touch anything, okay?"

Cody held his hands up. "No touch. Just look. Got it."

"Cool." Grant pressed the phone to his ear as he loped off.

"You're being pretty hard on him," Demetrius said.

"They forgot us at the airport. My own parents forgot to pick us up from the airport."

"They've been busy. It happens."

Cody growled low in his throat, and Demetrius's cock took notice. Damn, he wished they could find a few minutes to themselves. A quick blowjob might calm Cody down a bit.

"Why don't we go back to the house and see if we can find your mom and dad? They can show us where we're sleeping and we can get all settled in and then go for a walk in the snow."

"We walked through snow to get out here and see the pot plants."

"I'm trying to make this better for you." Demetrius gently shook his arm. "Work with me, all right?"

"Fine. Let's leave Grant to his call with Flick."

"His name's Fleck." Demetrius caught the glare from Cody and cleared his throat. "Sorry. He's now known as Flick."

Cody led the way back to the door, and they stepped out of the greenhouse and into the small entry foyer. Moments later, Grant exited the greenhouse as well.

"All done with the tour?" Grant asked.

"Yeah. We saw all the pot plants you're growing. We're going back to the house and see if we can find mom and dad and find out where we'll be sleeping."

"Oh, I can tell you that. I'll come with you."

They all changed out of coveralls and put on their outwear, then followed Grant outside. Demetrius trudged along the shoveled path behind Grant and Cody toward the house. The mountains looked deceptively close-by, sunlight gleaming off their granite skin and layers of snow. Demetrius paused to look all around him, taking in the hardwood and pine trees lining the back of the property and the snow-covered hillocks. Everywhere he turned, the mountains dominated the view.

On the ride in, the Uber driver had his radio tuned to a local news station, and the weather report had predicted another foot and a half of snow by Christmas. A foot and half more snow would put it up to Demetrius's waist, even higher with drifting. It was exciting and frightening at the same time. He just hoped they wouldn't get snowed in. He didn't think Cody or his family members would survive something like that.

"Demmy?"

Cody's voice pulled him out of his appreciation of the view and he caught up with them.

"Doing okay?" Cody asked.

"Just taking in the view."

"Never gets old," Grant said, smiling as he turned in place to look at the line of mountains. "So majestic. So breathtaking. So permanent."

"Yeah, they're big all right." Cody gestured toward the house. "Can we continue?"

"Oh, you're not staying in the main house." Grant shrugged. "Roman, Dave, and Brady and their families are all staying in the main house. You and Dems are going to stay with me out in the apartment."

"The apartment?" Cody started to say something more, but he stopped himself. He threw his hands up and said, "Of course. Why not? Show us the way."

"It's going to be like old times, Codes. Just hanging out and talking about stuff, getting to know each other again. You'll see. And Mac really wants to get to know you better, too."

"Can't wait to see her again," Cody said. "Last time I saw her, she had hair, so I'm sure we'll have a lot to talk about."

He followed Grant as he set off on the driveway plowed

through the deep snow, and Demetrius brought up the rear. They walked toward a two-story, three-car detached garage. Windows above the garage doors glowed with light, and Demetrius saw a couple of silhouetted figures pass before one of them.

Grant and his family lived in an apartment over the garage, and he and Cody were going to be staying with all five of them, including Mac, Grant's bald-headed girlfriend. Demetrius wondered how many more unexpected things were going to happen on this trip.

They tromped up a set of well-salted wooden steps on the side of the garage, and Grant led the way into the apartment. They stepped into a small mudroom and paused to remove their outer wear. Demetrius heard a TV and a couple of kids talking from other rooms.

"Our guests have arrived," Grant called.

A woman stepped into the doorway and smiled at them. "Welcome."

She was a bit taller than Demetrius, possibly six feet, and was in amazing shape, with broad shoulders and a flat stomach. A form fitting long-sleeved workout shirt showed off the muscles in her arms, and black leggings hugged her strong legs. The overhead lights gleamed along the skin of her scalp.

"Codes, you remember Mac," Grant said after he'd given her a kiss on the cheek. "And, Mac, this is Demetrius, my brother's best friend since elementary school. You can call him Dems."

"Don't call him that," Cody said before he gave Mac a brief hug. "Good to see you again, Mac. I like your hair style."

"It's so much easier in the morning." Mac smiled at Demetrius. "Welcome to our home. We're all so glad you both could make the trip."

"Could have fooled us by the reception," Cody said. "But, bygones. Where's our stuff?"

"Oh, it's still at the main house," Grant said. "We can get it later when we have dinner."

"May I use the bathroom?" Demetrius asked.

"Sure, it's down the hall, third door on the left." Mac gestured toward a doorway that led to a living room.

Demetrius flashed a smile at Cody before he walked out of the kitchen. He saw a large screen TV angled in a corner of the living room, and a love seat and two recliners around it. Two boys and a girl were on the furniture, the girl with her long dark hair in braids like Grant, the boys' long hair in ponytails. Their gazes stayed fixed on the screen, ignoring his presence. He walked down the hallway, counting doors until he reached the bathroom and closed the door.

After relieving himself, Demetrius took a moment to stare at his reflection. Holy hell, what had he and Cody gotten themselves into by agreeing to this trip? And where had Mr. and Mrs. Bower gotten off to? His sense of unease had been growing with each passing hour, and he still needed to keep Cody from going into full meltdown.

When Demetrius returned to the kitchen, he found Cody and Grant in the mudroom, hurriedly getting back into their boots and coats.

"Where are you going?" he asked, hoping no one caught the slight panic in his tone. He did not want to be left here alone with Grant's family.

"Mom called and said Dad's truck was found off the road," Cody said. His eyes were so wide, Demetrius could see the white all around the iris.

Demetrius moved into the mudroom and pulled on his gear as well. "Your Mom wasn't with him?"

"No. Apparently she's been at the house this whole time." He shot Grant a withering look.

"Why didn't she greet us?"

"That's an excellent question. Maybe Alice will grace us with an answer."

Demetrius stuffed his feet into his boots and followed Grant and Cody outside. As the door closed behind him, he heard Mac say, "Good to meet you, Dems."

CHAPTER FOUR

Emotions battled for dominance inside Cody. Night gained ground across the snowscape as Grant drove more than a little too fast along the snow-packed two-lane road. The plows had done a good job clearing the majority of snow from the blacktop, leaving tall mounds piled along the shoulder. On occasion, the wall of snow outside his window would vanish and display a drainage ditch or a dizzying drop-off made "safe" by a metal guard rail.

Demmy took his hand and gave it a squeeze. Cody smiled across the dimly illuminated backseat and squeezed back.

"I don't know what your father was thinking, taking this road after such a heavy snowfall," his mother said.

Cody closed his eyes and struggled to keep silent. All the words he longed to shout at the back of her head would not help the situation. He needed to keep his head in check until everything was figured out.

But so many questions echoed around inside him. Why hadn't anyone remembered to meet them at the airport? If his mom had been in the main house the entire time Grant had been showing them around, why hadn't she come out to greet them? Where had his father been going this far from home? Why was Grant acting suspicious about all of that? And where were his other brothers?

"You holding up okay?" Demmy asked.

Cody didn't think Grant and his mother heard because they were talking about the road and Cody's father's truck and the icy conditions and the weather report. Cody's smile felt tight, and he knew it didn't look convincing.

"I'm doing great. Aren't you glad you came along?"

Demmy took his hand again and held tight. "I wouldn't want to be any place else."

"Smooth talker."

"Learned it from the best."

"Amelia?"

They shared a chuckle.

"No, smart ass, you."

Grant half turned and said over the seat, "I see police cars up ahead."

Demmy released Cody's hand and they both shifted position to look through the windshield. The flashing lights painted the tall snow banks with staccato red and blue. Two state police cars and an ambulance blocked one lane. A cold, tight feeling in Cody's chest made it hard for him to breathe and the pulsing lights played havoc with his eyes.

"Oh my god, there's an ambulance," his mother said. "Is he in it? Do you see him?"

"I don't see him," Grant said as he stopped behind the ambulance. They all got out, and Cody gasped at the bite of the wind as he hurried to catch up to his mother. He linked his arm through hers and forced her to slow down.

"This road is icy," he told her. "Be careful."

"Where is he?" She craned her head side to side, trying to see around the emergency vehicles. "Where's his truck? Do you see it?"

Cody looked at her in the harsh play of lights, taking in her lithe frame and the brown hair gone mostly gray and pulled back into a loose knot at the base of her neck. The wind ruffled the fur trim of the hood of her parka and played with loose strands of her hair. At that moment, she looked significantly older than sixty-two, and the tension in her voice and expression played on Cody's empathy. The tight knot of anger in his chest loosened, and he turned his mother to face him.

"Mom, stay here with Grant. I'll go find someone to talk to."

"I should go," she said. "Let me. They know me, know us."

"You're kind of walking an emotional edge right now, okay? Let me go find someone." He moved her back a few steps until she stood with her back against Grant. Cody pulled her hood up over her head before he looked at Grant. "Keep her here and make sure she keeps her hood up. It's freezing out here."

"Okay, Codes."

Cody ignored the nickname and strode along the heavily packed snow lining the shoulder. He heard steps behind him and turned, ready to really lay into his mother. But the reprimand died when he saw Demmy.

"Thought you could use a second set of ears for this."

"Absolutely. Come on."

The wall of snow ended, leaving just the guard rail along the far edge of the road's gravel shoulder. Cody saw a gap in that guard rail just beyond the ambulance and police cruiser. He stopped and stared at the jagged ends of metal, saw the tire tracks through the crusted snow, and wondered how far his father had plummeted.

"Want me to look for someone?" Demmy asked.

Cody shook his head. "No. I'm... It's a little shocking, that's all. Come on."

A young trooper came around the front of his cruiser. "Hold up, you can't be here. This is an accident investigation."

"My father's down there. I'm Cody Bower, and we got a call that his truck had gone off the road."

"All right, I'll get the sergeant. Just wait here."

"Is he okay?" Cody asked. "Is he awake?" He couldn't bring himself to ask anything else.

"Let me get the sarge."

"Shit," Cody whispered as the trooper turned away and tipped his head to speak into the microphone clipped to his shoulder. "Shit, shit, shit, shit, shit."

"We don't know anything yet," Demmy said. "Let's wait until we hear what they know."

Cody inched closer to the guard rail, lifting his chin to see over it and down the other side. At least his father had gone off on this side of the road instead of the edge of the mountain.

"What'd he say?"

His mother and Grant stood directly behind him, making both him and Demmy jump.

"I told you to keep her back there," Cody said as he glared at Grant over their mother's head.

"I'm not a child," she snapped. "I want to know what happened to my husband."

"Cody..." Demmy gripped his elbow, and Cody turned to see a man approaching.

He'd probably once been in good physical shape, but had let himself go. His chest was broad and his belly big, and he walked with a slight limp that made Cody wonder if he'd been injured in the line of duty.

"Alice, I'm sorry to see you under these circumstances." The sergeant's voice was high and squeaked a bit, as if he'd just been sucking on a helium balloon. It was such a contrast to his physical appearance, Cody nearly let out a surprised bray of laughter.

"Mickey, just tell me the truth. Is he alive?" She squeezed Cody's hand hard, and when he looked down, he saw she had hold of Grant's hand as well.

"Hard to say for sure," Mickey said.

Cody frowned. "What's that mean?"

"He's not inside the truck."

"What?" His mother let go of both of them and stepped toward the sergeant. "Was he thrown clear? How much damage is there? Did you find any blood?"

"We found a little blood on the air bag, but nothing that looks like he sustained a serious injury. His phone was in the footwell of the passenger seat, but there's no other sign of him."

"You've looked all over down there?" Cody asked. "Like, all over?"

Mickey frowned. "Who are you?"

"Oh, this is our son, Cody. Cody, this is Sergeant Mickey Hastings."

"Sorry, I don't mean to suggest you haven't done your jobs. I'm very worried about my dad."

"I understand, son. And, to answer your question, we did look, like, all over." He looked back at Cody's mother. "There's not much searching we can do tonight. The wind is up and the snow is drifting, so even if he was mobile and able to walk away, his tracks would have been covered."

"Any idea what would have made him leave the road?" Demmy asked.

Mickey squinted in his direction. "You're too short to be a Bower. Who're you?"

"Oh, um, Demetrius Singleton, sir. I'm a friend of Cody's."

"I see." Mickey glanced at Cody before looking at his mother while answering Demmy's question. "There may have been some kind of impact prior to Greg going down the embankment. We'll be able to find out more once we pull the truck up out of the ravine. The wrecker should be here any time now. You're welcome to wait, but I would suggest you do so inside your vehicle. Do you have enough gas to start the engine and run the heater every few minutes?"

"Yeah, I filled up this morning," Grant said.

"Very good. Go back to your vehicle and wait for me to come get you. It might be a little while yet, so be patient."

They lingered a little longer until an especially bitter gust of wind drove them all back to Grant's truck. Cody got into the backseat with Demmy, and they all took some time to blow into their hands to warm up.

"How well do you know Mickey?" Cody asked.

"Oh, just from seeing him in town and whatnot," his mother said, turning her head briefly. He sat directly behind her, so she wasn't able to make eye contact.

They waited in tense silence as the wrecker pulled up. The emergency vehicles had to shuffle around to make room, forcing Grant to back up several yards. The troopers blocked traffic as the driver angled the wrecker properly. People slowly rolled past, stretching their necks to see what was going on.

It took nearly two hours to pull the truck up from the ravine. As the taillights rose into view, they all got out and huddled together to watch. Demmy whispered to Cody that he needed to pee and slipped away into the dark. Cody watched him go, feeling bad for what this trip had suddenly turned into. When they'd hung out together during their school years, they usually did it at Demmy's parents' because the Bower house was constantly in some kind of uproar with five boys spanning a variety of ages.

Demmy's house, by comparison, had been a quiet and serene setting. Cody had to temper his natural tendency of shouting to be heard above his brothers. They had spent hours in Demmy's room talking and laughing, reading comic books, playing video games, or watching movies without interruption or threat of attack from an obnoxious sibling.

Because of all this, Demmy hadn't been exposed to the full force of Cody's family very often. When he had stayed for an occasional dinner or sleepover, by the time he left he always seemed a little shell-shocked or worn down by the constant turmoil.

And here they were, spending time with Cody's family and trying to keep their heads above water as they navigated the usual storm. All of this chaos would ruin Christmas for Demmy. He should have known what to expect from this trip and convinced Demmy to stay back in Parson's Hollow where he'd enjoy a quiet, peaceful Christmas with Amelia and Otis and get some time to himself.

"Oh my god, look at the front end," his mother said.

He winced as the wrecker brought the truck through the broken guard rail. They saw the crumpled front end in the spotlights from the police cruisers.

"Jesus, that looks bad," Grant whispered.

Cody worked hard to keep his voice even and firm as he said, "Dad always wore his seatbelt, so he should have been okay. At least he used to wear his seatbelt."

His mother nodded, her gaze fixed on the truck and gloved hands clasped tight beneath her chin. "Always. He insisted we all do it, too."

"So, if he's not strapped into the seat, it's a good sign he was alert enough to get out."

"Unless he got thrown out," Grant said. Cody had to restrain himself from punching him in the head.

"What if that happened?" His mother turned worried and tear-filled eyes on Cody. "What if he's lying in the snow at the bottom of the ravine, freezing to death?"

"Mickey said they looked for him down there, remember?" Cody replied. "They didn't see any sign of him."

"What if they didn't look far enough? What if they stopped just feet from where he's lying?"

"Mom, you can't do this. You're going to make yourself crazy."

Mickey approached, his expression grim and his hands on his gun holster.

"As you can see, the damage is extensive, but the air bag deployed and the seatbelt was intact."

"What's that mean?" Cody asked.

"Means the seatbelt wasn't torn or pulled from the base. Makes me think he was awake and able to get out of the truck."

"Could he have been thrown out of it?" Grant asked. "Like, tossed?"

Mickey shrugged. "Maybe. But we looked and haven't seen any sign of him. Unfortunately, the wind is up tonight, and it gets trapped in these shallow ravines along the road. It spins around down there and whips the snow into mini-squalls that cause a complete white out and erases any tracks we might be able to follow."

"So he could be lying down there, covered with snow and freezing to death while we speak?" Cody's mother pulled free of him and pushed past Mickey, running toward the busted guard rail.

"Mom!" Cody ran after her.

"Alice, you can't go down there," Mickey shouted.

Cody caught her by the arm just as she reached the guard rail. He pulled her back against him, and they both stared down the slope. The tracks left by his father's truck as it had been hauled up were already starting to fill in as the wind howled through the ravine.

"Oh god," his mother said, sobbing with her face in her

hands. "Oh, Greg. Where are you?"

"Come on, Mom." Cody put his arm around her and led her slowly back to where Grant and Demmy stood waiting.

"Anything?" Demmy asked.

Cody shook his head. "Just pulled the truck up, as you can see." He handed his mother off to Grant. "Get her into the truck. We'll be there in a minute."

"Okay. Sure, Codes." Grant put an arm around his mother's shoulders and they went back to his truck.

"So, no sign of him?" Demmy asked.

"Mickey said it looked like the seatbelt was intact, so they're thinking he managed to get out of the truck and wander off. But the wind is blowing the snow around in the ravine and covering up any tracks."

"What do you think?"

Cody sighed and looked back at his father's truck where it sat on the side of the road. "I don't know, Demmy. That truck is busted to shit, but my gut is telling me Dad's still alive. But why didn't he climb back up to the road or take his phone with him for fuck's sake?"

"Yeah."

Cody thought Demmy's answer was pretty weak. Demmy pressed his lips together and looked at the ground, then back at Grant's truck where Cody's mom and brother sat in the front seats. Demmy looked at the crumpled front end of Cody's father's truck, and then held up a finger.

"I want to look at something."

Cody followed Demmy to the driver's side of his father's truck.

"Don't you boys touch anything," Mickey said from where he stood talking to the driver of the wrecker. "We're going to tow it back to the station and look it over in the shop."

"I just want to look," Demmy said. "I won't touch anything."

Demmy clasped his hands behind his back and leaned in close to the driver's door. Since Demmy was doing a close up view, Cody decided to take a couple of steps back and look at the bigger picture. The driver's side had considerable damage, including a large dent in the middle of the door Cody wrote off to the truck striking a tree on the way down the ravine. That would explain the missing side mirror as well.

When Demmy stepped back to Cody's side, he glanced over at him but didn't say anything.

"What are you thinking?" Cody gestured toward the truck. "You see something?"

Demmy hesitated then faced him. "You're going to be mad."

"What the fuck are you talking about?"

"If I tell you what I'm thinking, you're going to be mad."

"I don't understand what you're saying. If you have an idea about what happened to my dad, just tell me. Why would that make me mad?"

"Okay, but just remember you said that." Demmy grasped Cody's elbow and moved him toward the truck. "Look at the spot where the side mirror used to be."

Cody leaned in close. The arm supporting the side mirror had snapped off, leaving ragged metal behind. Something dark and coarse had been caught on the points, waving in the gusting wind.

"Hair?" Cody looked back at Demmy. "You think that's his hair?"

Demmy shook his head. "It's too coarse. It's animal hair. And also a bit of blood."

Cody inspected the area again and nodded. "Yeah, I think you're right."

"There's more."

"Okay, show me."

"Back this way."

As they walked past the driver's side of the truck, Grant powered down his window.

"You guys ready to head back to the house?"

"In just a few minutes," Demmy said. "I want to show Cody something."

"Okay, Dems."

Before Cody could complain about the most irritating nickname he'd ever heard, Demmy was already past the back of the truck, walking along the side of the dark road. Cody hurried to catch up.

"Where we going?"

"I walked a few yards back to find a place to pee."

"I really hope you're not going to show me you were able to spell your name in the snow, because it's really not the time for that."

"No. I found something."

"Yeah? A portapotty?"

Demmy stopped and stuck out an arm to keep Cody from passing him. "No. This."

Cody looked down at the ground where Demmy pointed. He frowned and dropped into a crouch, dangling his hands between his thighs as he got a closer look. The wind gusted, blowing loose snow across the ground and out of the deep impression in the hard-packed snow. An anxious, angry feeling started to swirl within him, and he clenched his jaw as he stood up again.

"Is that…?"

"I think so?"

"So, you're saying my dad hit bigfoot and went off the road. And then what? It grabbed him out of the truck and carried him off?"

"I don't know. I hope not. I just thought you should see it, and we could decide what to do."

Cody looked at the stars with his hands on his hips. He blew out a long, frustrated breath as he thought about everything Demmy had found.

"We've got another fucking monster case on our hands, don't we?"

"I wish I could tell you no with one hundred percent certainty."

"Fuck Colorado." He looked at Demmy and shook his head. "You know? Fuck Colorado, and fuck my family."

"What do you want to do?"

"I'm not telling Mickey the helium-sucking sergeant about this, that's for sure."

Demmy chuckled, then covered his mouth with a hand. "Sorry. I know it's not a humorous time. But what is up with that guy's voice?"

"I know, right?" Cody looked down at the large footprint. Even in the moonlight, he could tell it had been perfectly formed in wet snow that had frozen soon thereafter. He shook his head and crouched down again, pulling out his phone and snapping several pictures of it.

He walked back to his father's truck and took pictures of the hairs. Cody wasn't about to tell any of them what he was doing. Let them figure it out. He and Demmy were the experts in this kind of shit, and it was a damn good thing they'd both made the trip.

They got into the backseat of Grant's SUV and the heat felt glorious.

"What were you doing out there?" Cody's mother asked.

"Just looking around," Cody said. "I wanted to check some stuff out."

"What did you take pictures of?"

"A dent on Dad's truck and a spot in the road where he might have swerved. Mickey and his guys will see it all when they do the investigation."

"You ready to go now?" Grant asked, catching Cody's eye in the mirror.

"Yeah."

As Grant pulled onto the road, Cody's mother sighed heavily. "Oh god, I can't take talking to Felicia right now."

"What?" Cody sat forward and poked his head between the front seats. "Grandma Felicia? Why would you think about her?"

"She's your father's mother, Cody. Someone's going to have to tell her."

"Tell her what?" Cody said, his voice louder than he'd intended. "She's in a nursing home back in Parson's Hollow. She barely recognizes me, and I go see her once a week. No one needs to call Grandma, okay? And if it comes to that, I'll call her and talk to her. Just relax and let the police look for Dad."

"All right, you're right." She looked out her window, slowly shaking her head. "Where could he be? Why did he leave the truck?"

Cody sat back and stared out at the snow-covered landscape, wondering pretty much the same thing. Demmy took his hand. Cody looked over long enough to give him a grateful smile, even as the hair on the mirror support and the large footprint in the snow took precedence in his mind.

Merry fucking Christmas.

CHAPTER FIVE

Demetrius followed Cody through the front door of his parents' house, grateful to be out of the cold. His thoughts were dark and jumbled, and he really wanted to talk to Cody privately about what they'd found on the road. Those hopes were dashed, however, when they discovered the living room packed with more Bower family members. While they'd been gone, Cody's three other brothers and their families had arrived. As Alice explained things, everybody seemed to have fifteen questions and twice as many opinions on what should be happening at that exact moment.

While the Bowers talked themselves in circles, Demetrius snuck off to use the bathroom. He tracked down his and Cody's bags and set them by the door, then found an unoccupied chair in a nearby corner and observed the family.

Cody's mother, Alice, had had five boys. Grant was the oldest, followed a few years later by Roman, who was followed by Cody, then Dave and, finally, Brady. All five were over six feet, with Brady beating out Cody's six foot five by at least two more inches. Looking at them all towering over their slender and petite mother, Demetrius wondered how Alice had managed to survive giving birth to them.

"Who do I have to call to get a search party together?" Roman said. "Just give me the number, and I'll make the call."

Roman, the most conservative of the Bower boys, was very take charge and either assertive or aggressive, depending on Cody's mood. All Demetrius knew about Roman was that he lived in Utah with his wife, daughter, and son, he worked as some kind of investment banker, and he held very conservative views.

"You can't just order around a police department, Roman."

That statement came from Dave, the next in line after Cody, and the brother Cody was closest to. Cody spoke with Dave the most, and they often shared funny emails and text messages. Dave had lost some weight since Demetrius had last seen him, and he wondered if Cody had encouraged him to do it.

"Mom and Dad pay their salaries," Roman said, the volume of his voice rising on each word. "They work for us."

"None of us work for you, how many times do we have to remind you?"

That had been Brady, the youngest. He was hovering protectively close to a very pregnant and pretty blonde woman who sat on a love seat across the room. Her legs were stretched out, shoes off, and she slowly rubbed her hands over her abdomen.

"I didn't say any of you worked for me, you idiot. I said the police department does."

"I thought you said they worked for Mom and Dad?" Grant asked as he delivered noogies to the three kids Demetrius had seen up in their apartment.

Roman groaned. "That's not the point, dammit. What are they doing to find Dad?"

"Nothing they can do tonight, Roman," Cody said. "It

started snowing pretty hard as we left the scene of the accident."

"Grandpa's going to die?" asked a pretty young girl with long, dark red hair and features so fine and perfect she could have been a teen model.

"No, honey, it's just adults talking in abstract terms," said a similarly pretty woman with hair the same color and nearly identical style. "It's been a long day of travel for us. Let's get you and your brother settled into bed. Alice?"

Cody's mother looked lost and exhausted, her eyes full of tears and her face drawn. "Sorry, Madison. What did you say to me?"

"Where did you have the kids sleeping?" Madison asked. "And Roman and me?"

Alice shook her head. "Oh, sorry. I'm sorry. What a terrible hostess I've been."

Grant stepped forward, and Demetrius felt a warm affection for him as he took over for Alice. "I'll show you where Summer and Brock and you and Roman can set up camp. How was the flight?"

"Bumpy," said a young boy. He had hair the same color as his sister's, and he looked up at Grant with big eyes and said, "Your hair looks like a girl's hair," as he tugged a backpack up on one shoulder and followed his uncle out of the room.

"I think I'll go lie down as well," the very pregnant woman said.

Brady helped her off the love seat, and gave her a gentle kiss as he rested a hand on her belly. "Want me to come with you?"

"No, you stay here with your family. I'm fine, just tired." She stopped to give Alice a kiss on the cheek.

"Sleep well, Hilari dear. You take good care of that baby."

"I am, Mother Alice. You take care of yourself, too."

Demetrius was about to excuse himself to go out to

Grant's apartment when Cody caught his eye. Cody gave an exaggerated eye-roll and shook his head. Demetrius pointed at their bags near the door.

"Who's that?" Roman said, approaching Demetrius. "Who are you here with?"

"For fuck's sake, Roman, back off," Cody said, grabbing Roman's arm and tugging him back a couple of steps. "That's Demetrius."

"Demetrius?" Roman frowned and looked between them. "That skinny gay kid you hung out with in school?"

Heat flooded Demetrius's face, and he wished he could just drop into the floor and disappear. He'd never been described in such a succinctly homophobic way before. At least not to his face.

"What the fuck is wrong with you?" Cody gave Roman's shoulder a shove and stepped in close. "Demmy is my best friend, and we now run a business together. You'd know that if you read any of my emails, which apparently you haven't. And even if he was just some guy we happened to know around town, you still owe him an apology you rude bastard."

"Get out of my face." Roman tried to shove Cody back, but he'd planted his feet and didn't budge.

"Apologize."

"Fuck off."

"Boys! Enough!"

Alice's voice broke as she shouted and clapped her hands together twice.

Cody gave a very quiet growl before stepping away from Roman, and the sound of it struck Demetrius. The way Cody had stood up to his brother in his defense had been so fucking hot. Dammit, if only they could get an hour or so to themselves. But that kind of thinking needed to stop, because the rest of the family was staring at him.

He gave a small wave. "Hi, everyone. Yes, it's me, Demetrius, the skinny gay kid who hung out with Cody all through school. I must admit, I've never really heard myself described so quickly and precisely, so kudos to you on that achievement, Roman. Anyway, I know this is a difficult situation for everyone, but I think Cody and I are staying out in Grant's apartment, if I'm not mistaken?"

Demetrius raised his eyebrows as he looked around and finally found Grant where he had just returned from showing Roman's family to a guest room.

"That's right, Dems. You and Codes are bunking with me and my fam out in the apartment. Want me to walk you back?"

"Nope. No need. I can get there. I'll just leave you all to discuss the best plan of action with regard to your father. Just know I'll do everything I can to help out." He looked at their still expressions and staring eyes and lifted his hand in a quick wave. "Good night."

Demetrius picked up his bag and carried it a few feet to the front door. He almost fell a couple of times as he tugged on his boots, all while everyone in the room stared at him in silence. When he finally managed to get his feet into his boots, he pulled on his coat, hat, and gloves, picked up his bag, and slipped out into the cold wind and stinging crystals of the snow squall.

"Holy fucking hell," he grumbled as he trudged through the snow around the corner of the house. It was difficult to see in the storm, but he managed to pick out the lights of the garage apartment and headed in that direction.

He hadn't seen Grant's bald-headed girlfriend, Mac, in the living room, so he assumed she was at the apartment and, hopefully, not sleeping. Their trip, the storm, and the two-hour time zone difference had him completely confused as to what time it might be.

The wind bit every inch of exposed skin, even slipping up his sleeves and raising gooseflesh along his arms. By the time he marched up the steps to the door, Demetrius was shivering and nearly dead on his feet. The stress of Mr. Bower's accident site along with the intensity of watching the family talk about the crash had worn him out.

He knocked several times, and when Mac didn't answer, he tried the knob. The door was open, so he stepped quickly inside. After a pause to catch his breath, Demetrius slowly peeled away his protective layers and stepped into the kitchen in his stocking feet. Someone had left the light over the stove on, and it lit a path to the living room. There, he found two sleeping bags laid out on top of foam mattress pads and figured that was where he and Cody were going to sleep.

Not a lot of privacy for the next few days. Well, they could always look forward to New Year's Eve back home in Parson's Hollow.

Demetrius quietly dug through his suitcase for his toiletries and boxers and t-shirt to sleep in. The bathroom was clean and tidy, and he took his time brushing his teeth, washing his face, and relieving himself. This might be the last time he would be able to linger in a bathroom the entire trip, so he savored the moment.

Once he returned to the living room, Demetrius chose the sleeping bag closest to the tall windows looking out from above the garage doors. He could see the backsides of both the house and the greenhouse. How had Grant referred to it? Hemp House? Sounded more like a Nathaniel Hawthorne or Henry James novel. He knelt on the recliner in front of the window and rested his elbows on the back, watching the snow blow past a floodlight on the corner of the garage. He shivered a bit, chilled in just his T-shirt and boxers, but he wanted to wait up for Cody a while. A yawn snuck up on him, then another, and he couldn't fight it any longer. It had to be late, but he'd neglected to check the time while getting ready for bed.

He found his phone in the pocket of his coat and checked the display. Eight forty-five p.m. Well, that was embarrassing. Oh well, it was two hours later back home, and the long day would most likely be followed by even longer and more stressful days as they searched for Cody's father. Time to get some sleep.

The interior of the sleeping bag was surprisingly warm, with a hot water bottle tucked inside. Grant's girlfriend seemed to have thought of everything. He wondered if she went to bed early, then lost his train of thought to another big yawn. He snuggled down into the depths of the sleeping bag and positioned the hot water bottle against the small of his back. It was perfect, and he soon drifted off to sleep.

HE AWOKE IN COMPLETE DARKNESS, taking a moment to remember where he was. He heard Cody's familiar deep breathing beside him, and he was glad he'd finally made it back to the apartment. Demetrius hadn't heard anybody returning from the house. He must have really been out of it.

Wind gusted around the apartment, and hard pellets of snow ticked against the windows. Demetrius rolled over and looked at the darkness outside, then jumped in surprise when light bloomed, illuminating the snow streaking past. Someone must have triggered the motion sensor floodlight on the corner of the garage.

Curiosity pulled him over to the window. The air in the room was cool, and he shivered as he knelt in the recliner and leaned his elbows on top of the backrest. It was difficult to see through the driving snow, but after a moment Demetrius was surprised to see a figure moving around the back of the greenhouse.

A big figure.

It was very tall and broad as it slogged through the deep drifts. Its arms hung low, swinging back and forth as it walked. Snow clung to the dark, shaggy hair covering its body.

Chills chased up and down Demetrius's spine, and he gasped quietly.

The figure stopped mid-stride and turned its head toward the apartment. Snow covered much of the hair around its face, but left the eyes, nose, and mouth clear enough to see in the glare of the floodlight. The thing lifted its nose to scent the air, then it looked directly at Demetrius.

He ducked down into the chair, putting his head to his knees as he panted quietly. What the fucking hell had he just seen? It couldn't have been bigfoot stomping around the greenhouse. Could it? He had to wake Cody.

"Cody?" His voice was hoarse and barely carried in the still air. He cleared his throat and tried again, a little louder. "Cody. You need to see this."

No response. Demetrius slipped out of the chair onto the floor, crawling the short distance to the dark and lumpy form in the sleeping bag. He could hear Cody's deep, even breathing, and reached out to touch his shoulder.

The sleeping bag split apart and a terrifying roar filled the room. Demetrius jumped back as the monster he'd just seen outside burst out of Cody's sleeping bag. It grabbed for him with big, hair-covered hands, and its warm breath washed over him, stinking of rotten meat and dirt.

Demetrius jerked awake and lay very still inside his sleeping bag. His breathing and heart rate slowed as he gathered his senses. Just a dream, that was all. The sleeping bag was too warm now, and he fumbled with the zipper before throwing aside part of the upper layer. Cool air rushed in, and he felt around inside the sleeping bag until he found the hot water bottle. It had cooled, but he pulled it out and set it aside anyway.

Cody breathed deeply beside him, one arm outside of the sleeping bag and extended along the carpeted floor toward Demetrius. Moving slowly and quietly, Demetrius shifted onto his side facing Cody and watched him sleep. He liked waking up in the night and looking at Cody beside him. It was hard to believe sometimes that they were actually a couple, and Cody had "come out" to the rest of Parson's Hollow about their relationship. Demetrius had so often wondered what it was like to be one of Cody's girlfriends and on the receiving end of his affection and charm. And here he was, still making it work four months after they'd first gotten together.

And it was better than Demetrius had ever imagined.

The details of the dream had faded, but Demetrius could remember something happening outside, and he turned his head to squint toward the windows. Snow blew past practically sideways, illuminated in the glow of the floodlights beneath. Something must have triggered the motion sensor, but Demetrius didn't care enough to get up and see what. Plus he had an uneasy feeling about what might be out there.

Having cooled off, he pulled the sleeping bag back over him and burrowed in a little deeper. Tomorrow was going to be a very long day, and he really needed to get some sleep.

The sound of Cody's breathing helped him drift off, and he slept without dreams the rest of the night.

CHAPTER SIX

ody was living through his own personal hell.

Christmas music tinkled overhead as he shouldered his way through what could only be described as a wall of people. Bags slapped against his shins, the corners of the boxes inside poking and stabbing. He had one hand behind him, clutching Dexter, his brother Grant's youngest son. Dexter, in turn, held on to his sister Brooke's hand, and she held their half-brother Conrad's hand, who had very happily agreed to hold the hand of Summer, Roman's beautiful daughter. Summer held the hand of her brother Brock, who was holding onto Demmy.

It was all Cody could do not to stop in place and scream in frustration at the gaudily decorated mall ceiling.

He spotted a miraculously vacant table in a food court through an opening in the crowd and shifted direction. He dragged the kids and Demmy out of the mob of people, much to the displeasure of those shoppers surrounding him. Upon reaching the table, he directed each kid to a seat, and he and Demmy stared wide-eyed at each other across the table.

"I thought people bought all their gifts online," Demmy said.

"This is a freaking nightmare," Cody said.

"It's two days before Christmas," Summer said as she scrolled through an app on her iPhone. "Of course it was going to be crowded."

"Who needs food?" Cody asked.

All five kids and Demmy raised their hands. Great. This wasn't going to be difficult at all.

"I don't need you to buy my food," Conrad said, jerking his head to fling his long hair out of his eyes. He was thirteen and already full of teenage angst. "I can get my own food."

"Okay, so you'll be paying for it yourself, too?" Cody said.

Conrad's expression collapsed into sullen gloom, and he went back to whatever app he was looking at on his own phone.

"I'll take a few of you up to get food while Demmy and the others hold the table. When we come back, you guys can go. Sound good?"

Demmy smiled and nodded. "I like it."

"Thanks, Demmy. Okay, who's with me?"

None of the kids replied.

"If some of you don't come with your Uncle Cody, none of you eat."

Brooke and Dexter, Grant's kids, raised their hands, as did Brock, Roman's youngest.

"Perfect. Let's go, you three." He gave Demmy a tired smile. "Be back soon. Want me to get you anything?"

"I haven't decided yet. Good luck."

Cody gathered the three kids in front of him, and they headed toward the fast food counters. As he directed them through the crowd, Brooke tipped her head back to look up at him.

"Are you and Demmy boyfriends?"

Cody nearly tripped over his own feet.

"What? Why would you ask me that?"

"You offered to buy him lunch. That's something boyfriends do."

"Well, I'm going to buy you and your brother lunch. Does that mean I'm your boyfriend?"

She made a face. "No! You're, like, super old. Gross."

Cody furrowed his brow. "How old are you?"

"Ten."

"Want to make it to eleven?" he muttered.

"What?"

"Nothing. Hey, look, we've got lots of choices. What do you all feel like?"

Each kid shouted out a different restaurant and Cody groaned. Of course.

Cody handed out cash to Brock and Brooke, then got in line with Dexter, the youngest of the group. He watched the two older kids get in different lines, Brooke choosing a taco place and Brock a shawarma joint. What kid that age wanted a shawarma?

As he and Dexter waited in line, Cody thought about the morning-long family discussion that had led him to this point. With the kids occupied by a movie, the adults had all talked about his father's truck and lack of a body. Mickey had called early, according to Cody's mother, and had nothing new to report. The officers had searched for an hour before the storm became too much, but they'd found no tracks and no sign of Cody's dad.

Despite that, the kids all needed to be taken to the mall for the annual Christmas shopping trip. Roman's wife had a headache and needed to "lie in a quiet room," which Cody took to mean she needed her casket. Brady's wife was too pregnant to face the mall. Mac had to work at a nearby yoga studio, so everyone looked at him and Demmy. He'd protested, wanting to be out looking for his father, but his mother had said it would be a shame for the kids to miss out on the annual tradition, and it would also be a good chance for him to bond with his nieces and nephews.

Fine. So here they were at Ridgeline Mall, two days before Christmas.

As he waited in line behind Dexter for a burger, Cody felt his phone buzz with a text from Demmy.

You look really cute standing up there with Dexter.

Cody looked through the crowd to their table where Demmy sat grinning at him. He shook his head and sent back a response: *I am not putting a baby in you.*

Demmy wrote back: *Oh yeah? You've been trying to do just that an awful lot.*

Damn Demmy and his dirty mind. Or his ability to bring out the dirty thoughts in Cody's mind.

Before he could respond to Demmy's text, he and Dexter had to order. After he paid, he checked on Brooke and Brock and discovered each kid had already gotten food and gone back to the table. So much for sticking together.

When their food came up, Cody carried the tray through the crowd, keeping a close eye on his nephew who darted in and out of sight around people and tables. By the time Cody set down the tray, Brooke and Brock had already finished eating.

"Did you even taste your food?"

Brock shrugged. "The flavors weren't traditional, but it satisfied."

"How old are you?"

"Ten," Brock said, before his smart phone absorbed his attention.

Demmy chuckled as he got up to follow Conrad and Summer toward the food counters. Cody took a bite of his burger and felt immediate disappointment. He put it down and sent Demmy a text.

Don't get a burger. Worst burger ever.

Moments later, Demmy wrote back: *Thanks for the warning. Want me to get you something different?*

Cody grinned. *According to Brooke, you offering to buy me lunch means you're my boyfriend.*

I guess that makes it official then, Demmy wrote back. *Tell me what you want. Food, not sex.*

Cody surveyed the restaurant choices again and sent back an order.

"Who are you texting?" Brooke asked. She turned in her seat and looked toward the lines at the counters. "Demetrius just put his phone away. Were you texting with him?"

"I might have been. What's it to you?"

Brooke shrugged and looked at her phone. "Never mind."

Cody ate a few of his fries and tried to keep Brooke's question from getting to him. After Roman's reaction to seeing Demmy the night before, as well as Brooke's question about them being boyfriends, Cody was having trouble letting it go.

"Brooke."

She looked at him.

"Have your mom and dad said anything about me and Demmy?"

"I don't know. Not really." Back to the phone.

"Not really? What's that mean?"

Brock spoke without looking away from his phone. "My dad thinks you're gay. And he says Demetrius made you that way."

Cody clenched his jaw. Brock was Roman's kid, so Cody wasn't surprised by the flat and abrupt delivery of his statement. But Brooke was Grant's daughter, and he had been hoping Grant would be more laid back about things. He and his sons wore their hair in braids, for Pete's sake.

"That's not very nice, Brock," Dexter said around a mouthful of burger.

Brock shrugged and continued to stare at his phone.

Cody held out a hand. "Okay, that's it. Hand them over."

That got their attention. All three kids looked at him with big eyes.

"What?" Brock clutched his phone a little tighter. "Hand what over?"

"Your phones." Cody shook his hand. "Come on."

"Why?" Brooke asked. "We aren't making a fuss or talking too much."

"And that's exactly why I'm doing this. Give them to me."

"Brooke and Conrad only get their phones taken away when they've been bad," Dexter said. He looked at his sister. "Were you bad?"

"No!" She glared at Cody. "Why do you want our phones?"

"So we can talk to each other."

"You don't need to take our phones to talk to us," Brock said.

Conrad and Summer returned, each carrying a tray.

"Uncle Cody's trying to take our phones," Brooke said.

Conrad paled and stopped halfway down into his seat. "What? Why?"

"You have got to be kidding me. Are you all seriously that attached to your phones?"

"I don't have a phone," Dexter said. "I'm only eight. But when I'm ten, my dad says he'll buy me a phone."

"What did you do?" Summer glared at her brother, Brock.

"I didn't do anything!" Brock shouted.

Demmy arrived at the table. "Whoa, what's going on?"

"I asked for their phones."

"What were they doing?" Demmy sat in the chair beside him and handed over the two tacos he'd ordered.

"Nothing!" Brooke shouted, attracting the attention of people at surrounding tables.

"Okay, okay, calm down," Demmy said, and Cody could see him thinking things through. "Could there be some kind of compromise maybe?"

Cody ate one of the tacos in three big bites before he sat back and crossed his arms. "Like what?"

"Like maybe they all put their phones in their pockets while we're at the table?"

Cody grunted and looked around. The kids all stared back. He had no idea who these kids were. Sure, he knew their names and who their parents were, but he didn't know them. He had no idea what movies they liked or if they played sports. He didn't know their favorite subjects in school or any extracurricular activities. This trip could be his opportunity to get a glimpse into their lives. But first he needed to get them to look up from their phones.

But probably not the way he had tried to go about it.

"Yeah, that works," he said, then leaned forward and clasped his hands on the table. "I didn't mean I wouldn't give them back. You guys didn't do anything wrong. I just wanted us all to talk."

"Kind of a douchebag move, though," Conrad said. "Threatening to take away our phones."

"Hey, watch your language."

"You can't tell me what to do. You're not my uncle, because I'm not related to you."

"Does my brother feed and clothe you and put a roof over your head?" Cody asked.

Conrad scowled. "Yeah."

"Then he's acting like your dad, and I'm his brother, so technically, yeah, I'm your uncle and can tell you what to do. And, by the way, I'm also an adult and the leader of this little expedition, so there you go."

Cody pushed his chair back and stood up. He carried his tray to the nearest trash can and dumped the remainder of his burger and fries, but he held on to the surviving taco and his empty cup. It seemed like even more people had crowded into the food court since they'd sat down, and Cody threaded his way through the crowd to the soft drink dispenser at the burger place. While he waited in line behind a twenty-something guy trying to decide what flavor he wanted, Cody ate the other taco then looked back at the table. It seemed like Demmy and the kids were having a conversation, and he tried not to feel envious about that. Demmy always managed to smooth over any rough spots Cody left behind, and he was really good at making people feel comfortable. Even privileged and spoiled teens, apparently.

The guy finally chose Diet Dr. Pepper, and Cody had to cut him some slack for taking so long. At least he'd chosen well. When the guy moved out of the way, Cody stepped up and tried to fill his cup with Diet Dr. Pepper. The dispenser sputtered and fizzled as it released air and water. Of course.

"Your Diet Dr. Pepper is out," he said to the closest kid behind the counter. He got a blank look in return and impatiently pointed at the soft drink dispenser. "You're out of Diet Dr. Pepper."

"Oh, okay." The kid went back to ringing up his customer, and Cody watched him wait on others without telling anyone behind the scenes to change the tank on the Diet Dr. Pepper.

Fine. Screw it. He filled his cup with regular Dr. Pepper and stomped back to the table. He didn't sit down, but stood looking at the others who looked right back.

"All right. We've hit four stores so far," Cody said. "Which ones are next?"

"We're not going to talk?" Brooke asked, and damned if she didn't sound disappointed.

None of the kids held a phone, not even Demmy. Cody sat

down again and asked Demmy in a quiet voice, "Did you bribe them?"

Demmy grinned, and if he didn't look so damn cute doing it, Cody might have been annoyed. "Nope. Just told them you wanted to get to know them better because you don't get to see them very often."

"He also said you talk big and mean, but you're actually a big softie," Dexter said.

"Traitor," Demmy said.

"Fine." Cody took a long drink of soda before he smiled at the kids. "Let's talk."

"Where's Grandpa?" Brock asked.

Cody mentally strung every curse word together and let them run through his mind a few times in a row. Then he took a breath and said, "We don't know. His truck went off the road about half an hour away from the house. There was no sign of him at the accident site."

"Do the police think he's dead?" Summer asked.

"Didn't your folks talk with you all about this last night or this morning?"

They shook their heads.

"They told us they were all going to be busy, and that we'd do our Christmas shopping with you," Summer said.

"Well, that would have been nice to know before now."

"Do *you* think he's dead?" Conrad said, flipping his hair out of his eyes.

"No. I don't. But I am worried about him."

"Was there a lot of blood in his truck?" Brock asked.

"Just a little bit on the air bag, but not too much."

"What if he's hurt or has amnesia and is just wandering around in the snow?" Brooke looked at her cousins with a scared expression.

"Look, I grew up with your grandpa, okay? He's my dad, and I know him really well."

"My dad said you haven't seen Grandpa and Grandma for over five years," Conrad said, flipping his hair again.

Cody let himself hope the kid would get a muscle cramp in his neck, then squashed the thought. He was above being that petty. Maybe.

"Yeah, that may be true, but Grandpa raised me right along with your dad." He pointed at Summer and Brock. "And your dad and your other uncles."

"What about Demetrius?" Dexter looked at him. "Did he know Grandpa?"

"Oh, um, sure. I knew your grandparents. Uncle Cody and I have been friends since we were younger than you."

Dexter's eyes grew big and round. "That long?"

"Yeah, yeah, all right, settle down," Cody said. "We're not that old."

"You're pretty old," Summer said with a grin.

"Yeah," Brooke said. "Like, almost ancient."

"Hey now," Cody said, putting on an over-exaggerated hurt expression.

"Ancient aliens," Conrad put in. "That's you two."

"Okay, well, I've finished my lunch." Demmy stood up. "How about we do some more shopping?"

"I want to bake cookies," Brooke said.

"That's later tonight with Grandma," Dexter said.

Brooke nodded. "And Grandpa."

"Not if they don't find him," Conrad said.

Brooke and Dexter both looked on the verge of tears.

"Hey now, there's no need to get like that, Conrad," Cody said.

The kid shrugged and flipped his hair out of his eyes again. He was definitely going to give himself some kind of muscle spasm doing that.

While the kids dumped their trash, Cody stood next to

Demmy and wished he could kiss him or hold his hand or something.

"Thanks for the assist with the phone thing," Cody muttered.

"No problem, Uncle Cody." They both winced. "That just sounds way too creepy. I will never say it again."

"Thank you."

"How much longer do you want to stay here at the mall?"

Cody shrugged. "I'd leave now if we didn't have this list of gifts the kids need to buy."

Brock took Cody's hand. "I hope they find Grandpa soon."

"Me too, buddy."

"You said he was near the mountains?"

"Well, closer to the mountains. He was driving on a road with a lot of hills about half an hour from their house."

Demmy gathered the other four kids, and they set off into the crowd. Brock and Summer both pointed out a store that had science gadgets and brain teaser toys.

"Can we go in there?" Summer asked.

Cody checked out the other kids' expressions, surprised to see Conrad wasn't scowling. Then he caught a glimpse of Conrad sneaking a long, lingering look at Summer and understood.

Conrad was crushing on Summer. Cody couldn't blame him; she was a beautiful girl. But, it was wrong because they were first cousins. No, he corrected himself, she actually wasn't his cousin by blood. Conrad was the son of Grant's girlfriend, Mac, and a previous boyfriend. So, not blood cousins, but still kind of gross. Those two would need close watching.

The store was pretty empty, so Cody let out a breath and relaxed enough to let the kids wander the aisles on their own. He looked around for Demmy and found him standing in front of a two foot tall molded plastic figure of bigfoot.

"That guy's got some major back hair," Cody said when he walked up to him.

Demmy flashed a grin then looked around to see where the kids were and lowered his voice. "What do you think of what we found at the accident site?"

Cody shook his head. "I'm trying not to."

"Maybe your dad hit it as it was crossing the road, and that's why he crashed. And then he ran and left his phone behind because he was scared."

"Or it dragged him out of the truck into the snow. We know how these things operate."

"We've never gone up against a bigfoot before."

"Can I help you find anything?" asked a woman wearing a tag with the name BARB on it.

Demmy smiled. "Oh, no thanks. Just waiting for the kids to finish looking around."

"They're cute. Are they all yours?"

Cody nearly choked. "Ours?"

"Yeah. You looked so protective of them all when you first came in, I just figured they were yours."

"No, they're not ours," Demmy said. "We're just watching them for the day."

Barb nodded, then leaned in and lowered her voice. "Are you with the production team?"

"Which production team?" Cody asked.

"Some monster movie for one of those cable channels. They're filming all around this area, and I saw you admiring our friend here and just thought you might be involved somehow."

"More than you'll ever know," Cody muttered.

"What's that?"

"No, we're not part of the production," Demmy said quickly. "Do you know where they've been filming, though? My friend's father was in a car accident a little ways outside of town, and he's missing. They might have some information for the police."

Barb looked stricken, and she put a hand on her chest. "Oh, I'm so sorry to hear about your father. Do you have any information at all?"

"Not much, I'm afraid," Cody said.

"I don't know where the team has been filming exactly. They've been all over the area to get different places near the mountains and some houses on the outskirts of town, that kind of thing." She shook her head. "I do hope you find your father, and he's not injured."

"Thank you."

All five kids converged on them, each holding an item and smiling.

"We're done with our Christmas shopping!" Summer said.

"Wow, that's great you guys!" Barb led them all over to the register, and Cody looked at the bigfoot figure again.

"Fucking monsters," he muttered.

"You can say that again," Demmy said.

"I say it every time we get one of these cases, though it doesn't do much good."

"True. Come on, the kids are ready. Let's get back to the house."

Cody gathered up the kids and, with a wave to Barb, ushered them out of the store into the crowd.

CHAPTER SEVEN

W hen they arrived at Cody's parents' house, Roman's wife, Madison, was in the kitchen chopping vegetables and singing along to a high-pitched pop singer playing through her iPhone. Summer and Brock hugged their mother then ran off after the other kids. Demetrius said hello and sat on a stool at the island counter as Cody stood nearby.

"Any word about Dad?" Cody asked.

Madison shook her head and scooped some onions into a skillet where they sizzled in oil. "Nothing yet. I thought I'd make some chicken soup so we'd all have something to eat between shifts."

"You look like you feel better," Cody said. "Headache gone?"

"Yes, thank goodness. They always come at inopportune times." She chopped cilantro into small leafy bits.

"I'm sure." Cody tipped his head toward the front door, and Demetrius slid off the stool. "I guess we'll head to the apartment and see what we can do to help out the others."

"The kids get their shopping done?"

Cody nodded. "They're all set."

"I really appreciate you taking them. I hope they weren't too much of a handful for you. I know you're not used to having kids around." She glanced up at Demetrius as she chopped. "Either of you."

"They were good," Demetrius said. "They're great kids. You should be proud."

"We definitely are." She put down the knife and smiled at Cody. "So, any special girl in your life?"

"You know, I think I'll wait until the whole family is together before I talk about that," Cody said.

"Oh? Has there been a change from your usual love 'em and leave 'em ways?"

"You might say that. But I want to be able to tell everyone at once. Including Dad."

Madison nodded as her expression shifted from sly to something more appropriately contrite. "Of course. I look forward to hearing about your special girl."

"I'm sure. My Mom's not a big fan of cilantro, so you might want to take it easy on that."

Demetrius left the kitchen, and Cody followed him. They pulled on their boots and outerwear, then stepped outside, shivering in the cold and squinting in the bright sunlight as they headed for the garage.

"She's quite the inquisitor," Demetrius said.

"Yeah. She's always been like that. Their wedding was one of the most stressful events I've ever attended."

"I kind of remember you talking about it afterward. How long have they been married?"

Cody had to think about that. "About fifteen years, I guess."

"They seem perfect for each other," Demetrius said.

"Yeah. Bully for them."

Demetrius followed Cody up the steps to the apartment door. It was unlocked, and they stopped in the mudroom to remove their boots and coats. They walked through the apartment and found it empty, then stood in the living room looking at each other.

"No one home," Cody said, waggling his eyebrows.

"The kids are all at your parents' house, and they could show up at any minute."

"Spoilsport."

"Just trying to keep from traumatizing a niece or nephew."

"Yeah, yeah." Cody headed for the kitchen. "Let's see what big brother Grant has to eat and drink."

"You don't want to call your mom or one of your brothers and check on how the search is going?"

"If there was any news, they'd get in touch."

Demetrius studied Cody as he searched through the fridge. After a couple of minutes, Cody looked over his shoulder and caught him watching. "What? Change your mind about fooling around?"

"What's going on?"

Cody closed the refrigerator door. "I'm pissed off is what's going on."

"Yeah, but your dad is missing. Shouldn't we be out there helping?"

"I have no idea where they are or what they're doing. They've completely shut me out of all of this, and it fucking hurts. Okay?"

"I get that, Codes." Cody grinned reluctantly. "Being with family is really difficult, especially around the holidays. But you know what's a worse time to be around family? A funeral. Especially when we have information that may help the police find your father."

"I'm not going to the police and tell them I think bigfoot is responsible for my father's disappearance."

"Okay, then let's go out and help with the search ourselves but keep our eyes open for any kind of lead."

Cody grunted and crossed his arms. "We do have Grant's big SUV just sitting out there."

"We do. And if I remember last night correctly, he entered the nearest intersection to your dad's accident scene into the GPS."

Cody smirked. "This is one of the many reasons we've been friends for so long."

"Yeah? What's that?"

"You can be sneaky when the situation calls for it."

"Thanks?" Demetrius grinned. "We should dress in layers if we're going to be outside for long."

After getting properly dressed, Cody stopped by the main house to tell Madison they were going out for a bit. While Cody backed the big SUV out of the driveway, Demetrius played with the buttons on the large touchscreen in the dashboard until he managed to get to previous GPS routes.

"You're like some kind of secret agent," Cody said.

"I was just watching Grant use the GPS last night, that's all. Kind of amazed at all of these options."

"I was thinking this morning as I drove to the mall that maybe Grant is selling some of his product on the side to be able to afford a car like this."

"That or he's over his head in debt."

"Like us?"

They shared a grin, and Demetrius reached across the center console to take Cody's hand.

"I'm sorry the trip to see your parents has become so intense."

"Quite the cluster, isn't it?"

"You managing all right?"

"What do you think?"

Demetrius studied Cody's profile, noting the tiny lines of tension at the corner of his eye and the firm set to his jaw. "I think you're doing great, considering what we've had to do since arriving less than twenty-four hours ago."

"We haven't been here a full week yet?"

"Just feels that way."

They were quiet for a time, holding hands as Cody followed the GPS directions.

"Nice to see that Roman is still pretty much a dick," Cody said.

"Consistency does make some things easier."

"I'm sorry he said those things last night." Cody squeezed Demetrius's hand and glanced at him. "I do intend to tell them about us. But I want to wait until we find my dad."

"It wasn't the time last night," Demetrius said. "I completely understand."

And he did understand. Finding Cody's father was much more important than Cody telling his family about their relationship. The simple fact that Cody intended to tell his family made Demetrius feel secure and happy. He had no fear the Bowers could come between them. He knew how important he was in Cody's life, and Roman's homophobic comments and attitude weren't going to change that.

A short time later, Cody pulled the SUV off onto the shoulder behind a state police cruiser. Since they'd left the night before, the police had put up wood planks as a temporary guard rail in the spot where Cody's father's truck had gone through. Orange barrels stood at either end to warn drivers of the weaker barrier.

When they got out of the SUV, a state trooper stepped out of the cruiser and approached.

"Help you guys?"

"My father was the one who went off the road last night. We were hoping to join the search party." Cody looked up and down the empty two-lane road. "I don't see any other cars though."

"There's a gas station a few miles down the road where they all decided to park for safety's sake." The trooper pointed. "You can park your vehicle there and join them."

"Are you here to give people directions?" Cody asked.

The trooper shrugged. "Not really. I was here while the road crew put up the temporary guard rail. Was about to set off on patrol when you pulled up."

They thanked him and got back inside the SUV. Cody started the engine, but Demetrius put a hand on his forearm.

"Hold up a minute."

"What for?"

Demetrius watched the trooper pull out onto the road and drive off, then he opened his door and stepped out. He walked a short distance behind the SUV, his eyes cast down as he looked for the footprint. The storm from the night before and what had probably been multiple passes from a snow plow had obscured it.

Cody came up alongside him. "Find it?"

"No. Too much new snow and activity. Can I see the picture you took of it last night?"

Cody brought out his phone, and they looked at the photo. The flash had washed out much of the detail, but Demetrius could see the rough edges of the footprint. A bit of the guard rail had been captured in the picture as well, showing one of the wooden posts and the bolts securing the rail to it. From one of the bolts ran a long trail of rust down the aluminum guard rail, like a tear. Demetrius walked along the rail until he found that same post. The footprint was gone, wiped away by the storm and traffic. But when he looked at the woods on the other side of the guard rail, he saw a small gap in the trees.

"Look there." Demetrius pointed. "Is that a trail?"

"It could be." Cody stood close beside Demetrius and dropped down to one knee. He cleared away some of the loose snow, which only revealed hard-packed snow under-neath. "The snow plow definitely ruined the print."

"We could walk along this trail and see where it leads."

Cody stood up. "Who are you trying to find, my dad or bigfoot?"

Demetrius didn't really have a response. He had been thinking about following the trail and coming across bigfoot and getting pictures or some kind of physical proof. Guilt swamped him, and he blushed.

"You're right. I'm sorry. I lost track of what we should really be focusing on. Can I just get a picture of the mile marker here and the break in the trees?"

"Fine. I'll be in the truck."

Demetrius took a few pictures of the area before he hurried to the SUV and got inside. Cody pulled back onto the road and drove in silence.

"I'm really sorry about that. I know we need to focus on finding your father."

Cody was quiet long enough for Demetrius to wonder if he'd really just fucked everything up between them.

"I accept your apology. But it does open the door to a larger issue I think we need to discuss."

Chills crawled up Demetrius's back even though he wore so many layers. "Oh?"

The gas station came up on their left, and Cody pulled into the lot. Trucks and SUVs took up almost all of the parking spaces, and Cody pulled into one of the last remaining spots. He turned off the engine and sat looking at the center of the steering wheel. The longer Cody stayed quiet, the more Demetrius worried. He'd really fucked up suggesting they try to track whatever Cody's father may have hit rather than Greg himself. What he wouldn't give to be able to go back in time to the moment they'd pulled up behind the state police cruiser.

Just when Demetrius had screwed up enough courage to say something, Cody started talking.

"We've been involved in some pretty messed up stuff over the last year. And even though we've both been through a lot, I think we're in a really good place now."

Relief chased the chills from Demetrius, and he was quick to say, "I think so, too."

"But you seem to have developed this really strange obsession with these crazy cases we keep stumbling across."

"The first case was just a wrong place, wrong time thing," Demetrius said. "I mean, our clients were being murdered, so we had to figure that one out."

"Yeah, I get that. And the chupacabra we decided to get involved in because we needed the work."

"Right. And I had no control over the swamp monster. We had to find Amelia."

Cody waved a hand. "I know. And back in September I agreed to go along with you to look for the Pinesville Devil."

"The Devil of Pinesville," Demetrius said in a quiet voice. He smirked when Cody glared at him. "See how it feels to be corrected about those things?"

"Anyway…" Cody looked away and tapped a hand on the steering wheel. "I'm not sure what I wanted to say, but it just seems that you're, I don't know, excited about these cases now. Is this what you want our business to turn into?"

"I don't know." Demetrius felt a different sense of shame now. Had the mysterious and otherworldly paranormal cases drawn him in too far? "I have to admit that the few out of the ordinary cases we've worked on have been exciting. They're not the standard possum or raccoon removal, you know? And the way I look at it, we've saved some lives by getting involved."

"We've also gotten ourselves into very dangerous situations."

"That's true. But we've come through it all without serious injuries."

"Everything you're saying sounds so calm and normal and sane while we're sitting here in the car with the sun shining and people around us. But then we start digging into something like the possibility of bigfoot being involved in my dad disappearing, and things take a nasty turn. I don't want us to end up dead and never found because of some goddamn monster."

"I understand what you're saying. I don't want us to end up a meal for something huge and scary that lurks around woods or swamps either. How about we focus on helping the police find your dad, and then we just get through the holidays with your family and forget all about any possibility that bigfoot exists, let alone had a hand in causing the accident?"

"You think you can do that?"

"I will definitely do it." Demetrius gave a nod. "Come on. Let's get ready and find your family. No one's better at tracking down and capturing critters than the two of us. Just treat your dad like he's some rogue raccoon."

That got a small smile, and Demetrius felt a little better.

"Thanks for talking," Cody said. "Sorry if I snapped at you."

"You didn't snap. And considering what's going on, you're allowed a snap or two."

Cody did a quick check of the area, and then he leaned across the console for a kiss. "I missed sleeping with you last night."

"You were in the sleeping bag right beside me." Demetrius kissed him again, drawing it out a little longer this time.

"You know what I mean."

"I do. And I missed you, too."

One more kiss, and they got out of the SUV. Cody locked

it and zipped the keys inside a pocket of his coat. Demetrius pulled on his hat and gloves as they walked toward the back of the gas station parking lot. A couple of officers, a man and a woman, got out of a state police SUV as they approached. Demetrius recognized the man as the helium-voiced sergeant Cody's mother had introduced them to the night before.

"Help you guys?" the sergeant asked.

"Yeah, hi. We met last night. It's Mickey, right?" Cody said.

"Sergeant Hastings," he replied, adjusting his gun belt. "I remember you. It's Cody, right?"

"Mr. Bower," Cody said. Demetrius pressed his lips tight together to keep from laughing.

The sergeant looked between them before focusing on Cody once again. "What can we help you with?"

"We heard the search party for my father is headquartered here," Cody said. "We'd like to join in."

"They've been gone for a while now," the woman said. "A few hours."

"We couldn't make it until now," Cody said. "Can we maybe follow along after them as a second set of eyes until we catch up?"

Mickey and the woman looked at each other, and Demetrius feared they would be told no. But then the woman shrugged, and Mickey gestured for them to follow him. He gave each of them a number of plastic red flags on thin wires. Demetrius's flags all had the number 43 printed on them, and Cody's all had 44.

"Write down your names and mobile numbers on this sign-in sheet next to the number on your flags," Mickey said, handing Cody a clipboard.

Once they'd finished, the woman walked with them to the edge of the parking lot. A snow-covered field stretched away toward a group of pine trees growing among some big pieces of granite that looked to have burst up through the ground thousands of years ago. Tracks from the search party had completely trampled the pristine white surface of the field and knocked the snow off the lower branches of the pine trees.

"It'll get dark in a few hours. Follow the path already set by the search team. They headed toward a small animal run your dad may have taken. It's about a quarter mile through the trees. You'll probably run into them coming back. If you find anything you think deserves a second look, plant one of your flags next to it. Officers with the rest of the team will look at potential evidence. Don't disturb anything you come across. Is that clear?"

Demetrius and Cody both nodded.

"We've got your mobile numbers, and we'll take roll when the entire group comes back to make sure we haven't lost anyone."

"Have you heard from them at all?" Cody asked. "Have they found anything?"

She looked apologetic. "They haven't been in touch. You'd best get a move on, you're losing daylight."

"Story of our lives," Cody grumbled. "Let's go, Demmy."

They set off across the field. The packed-down snow crunched beneath their boots, and their breath steamed in the frigid air. Demetrius was glad he'd worn long johns beneath flannel-lined jeans. He'd probably work up a good sweat walking through the trees, but that was better than freezing.

"What's up with Sergeant Squeaky Voice?" Cody said. "Seems to have a chip on his shoulder with me, and I just met him."

"He did seem to have a problem with you," Demetrius said. "And I don't remember you doing anything to give him a reason for it."

Cody looked over his shoulder. "Are you suggesting I often give people a reason to take an attitude with me?"

Demetrius blinked and tried his best to look confused and innocent. "Sorry, what?"

"Humph," Cody said, turning forward again.

Demetrius stayed quiet and focused on looking for evidence. Cody seemed happy to have the conversation end, and Demetrius left him to his thoughts. Planning the trip had been stressful enough, and Greg going missing really ratcheted up the tension.

The animal run was a very narrow space that meandered through the trees, and they stopped and looked off in both directions. The search team had apparently split in two, one part heading toward the road and the accident site and the other following the trail deeper into the woods.

"Which way feels lucky?" Demetrius asked.

Cody looked right, then left, then right again. Finally, he shrugged and pointed straight ahead toward an even narrower gap between two pine trees.

"What do you say we take the animal run less traveled?" Cody said.

"Are you sure?" Demetrius looked over his shoulder, but the trees they'd passed blocked them from view of the officers at the gas station.

"No. But I'm going with my gut here. Want to follow my gut or the rest of my family?"

Demetrius gestured toward the unspoiled snow in front of them. "I've always liked your abs. Let's go with your gut."

Even though Cody's grin looked sad, Demetrius was heartened by it. He let Cody lead the way between the trees and into the woods.

CHAPTER EIGHT

Cody didn't think he'd made a mistake when he'd suggested they move off the beaten path to conduct their own search. But now that they were an hour from Mickey and the gas station parking lot, he'd noticed the sun was going down a lot faster than he'd anticipated, and it worried him a bit.

He stopped and leaned against a hardwood tree to catch his breath and looked back. Demmy had paused as well, propping himself against a different tree as he panted. His face was red, and sweat stood out on his forehead just beneath his hat.

"This deep snow is hard to walk through," Demmy said.

"This may not have been my best idea."

"Better than trying to skateboard down the road by holding onto the back fender of my bike."

Cody chuckled and flexed his knee. "I still have the scars from those scrapes."

"I'm very aware of every one of your scars." Demmy grinned and waggled his eyebrows.

"If I weren't afraid of passing out trying to peel off all your layers, I'd be all over you right now."

"You say the sweetest things."

Before Cody could suggest they turn back, he heard a sound. From Demmy's expression, he'd heard it too. Cody looked into the trees ahead of them. The sun was sinking fast, and the light played tricks with his eyes, making shadows seem to move. He held up a hand for Demmy to stay where he was and took three long, careful steps.

Something moved behind a tree about ten feet in front of him. It was tall and broad and looked like it was covered in hair.

Fucking hell. It could be a bear. Or Demmy might have been right about that footprint.

Cody started to look back at Demmy and motion for him to retreat, but the tall, broad, hairy figure moved. It faced away from them, shifting position as the muscles in its back flexed. It lifted its leg, pulling a massive foot out of the snow and planting it behind for better support.

And then it turned and looked over its shoulder right at him.

"Run!" Cody shouted.

He turned away from the thing—bigfoot, it's fucking bigfoot—and took off running. Demmy wasted no time asking what he'd seen. With everything they've been through, he had already turned and started running back the way they'd come.

Cody heard the thing rumble some kind of growl, and the sound urged him to move faster. Demmy was a few feet in front of him, high-stepping to clear the snow, both of them grunting and panting.

A mix of growls and snorts from behind sent shivers through him. He expected at any second to feel a big hand grab his shoulder and spin him around, and then the thing would choke him until it crushed his neck.

How far had they walked away from the wider animal run? It felt like they had been trying to escape forever.

He risked a glance back, and his heart hammered even faster.

The thing was bounding after them, the fur around its face dusted with snow, highlighting the simian appearance. It stretched out an arm, fingers clutching at him, but Cody was a few feet out of its reach.

"Faster!" Cody shouted.

Demmy looked back, his eyes big and his mouth a dark O of shock and exertion.

"What the fuck?" Demmy managed to shout between gasps.

"Just go!"

They burst out of the trees onto the animal run. Free of the thigh-deep snow, Demmy sprinted through the more widely-spaced pine trees and out into the open field. Cody was just a few feet behind him, and he could see people standing around the police cruisers in the gas station parking lot on the other side of the field.

He looked back and gasped with relief. The thing had not pursued them across the animal run. Cody could barely see its outline, glaring at him from behind a couple of trees.

Cody slowed a bit and managed to say, "Demmy... It's okay... It stopped."

Demmy looked back and then tripped over his own feet and went down on the snow. Someone in the parking lot called out, and Cody saw several people hurrying toward them. He reached Demmy and dropped to his knees beside him. They were both out of breath as they looked at each other.

"You okay?" Cody asked.

Demmy nodded.

"Codes? Dems? Dudes, what are you doing here?"

Grant stood grinning in the sepia-toned final moments of the day.

"We came to help," Cody said, finally managing to get his breathing under control. He looked back toward the trees, but the thing had slipped away. Of course.

His mother came up beside Grant. "We didn't see you out there."

"We looked in some different places." Cody pushed to his feet and extended a hand to Demmy to pull him up. "Not hurt?"

"Not hurt. You?"

"I don't think I'll be sleeping anytime soon, but I'm not hurt."

"You're both covered in snow. Let's get back to the house, and I'll make us all some cocoa," Cody's mother said.

"I've got some peppermint schnapps you can spike yours with." Grant winked.

"Come on, Dems," Cody said and put his arm around Demmy's shoulders. "We could both use some spiked hot cocoa."

"Do you think it was… You know?" Demmy asked in a low voice.

"From what I could see of it, yes."

"Did it look injured?"

"Injured? Why?"

"Like if your dad had hit it with his truck."

"Oh. Right. Well, it ran pretty damn fast, so I'd say if he did hit it, he didn't do much harm."

Demmy fell quiet as they reached the parking lot. They handed over the marker flags they'd miraculously kept hold of, then Cody passed Grant the SUV's keys. He noticed his mother talking with Mickey, both of them looking around anxiously. He watched them a moment until Mickey noticed him and indicated him with a quick jerk of his chin. Cody's mother looked at him over her shoulder, then turned her back on Mickey and hurried over.

"Let's get home, I'm nearly frozen through," she said.

"What was that all about?" Cody asked.

"What was what all about?"

"What were you talking with Mickey about?"

"He's Sergeant Hastings to the public," she said. "And we were just discussing what the department has done to find your father. Come on now, get in the front."

"What has the department done to find dad?" Cody asked.

"All they can. Come on. In, in, in." His mother got in the backseat between Roman and Brady, while Dave and Demmy sat in the third row of seats in the very back.

"How were the kids?" Roman asked.

"Kids were great," Cody said. "They all bought gifts, and we brought all four home safe and sound."

"Four?" Roman and Grant said together.

Cody grinned and stared straight ahead without replying.

"Douchebag," Roman muttered.

"Language," their mother said.

"Codes, that was awesome," Grant whispered. "Scared me for a minute, sure, but still, it was awesome."

IN HIS MOTHER'S KITCHEN, Cody managed to get Demmy off to the side as cocoa preparations were underway.

"That thing was seriously coming after us," Cody said.

"I didn't see much of it. Mostly your expression which was enough to get me to run."

"Felt like we were back in the swamp being chased by that

monster. Only freezing our asses off in deep snow instead of sweating our asses off in deep mucky water."

"We do seem to get chased by things a lot."

Dexter approached and tipped his head way back to look up at Cody.

"Hey Dex. What's up, little man?" Cody said.

"Are you two boyfriends?"

All conversation in the kitchen stopped. Cody's heart stuttered through the next few beats, and a slick layer of sweat broke out all over his body. He drew in a breath and saw his brothers and mother standing on the other side of the kitchen looking back at him. It seemed fitting, he supposed, that he and Demmy were on one side of the big marble-topped island with the stovetop and sink and his entire family was on the other. Perfectly staged for just this moment.

"Dexter, come here and help me out," Cody's mother said. "How many marshmallows go in each cup?"

"Uncle Cody hasn't answered my question yet."

"We don't ask those kinds of questions," Madison said as she hurried over and put her hands on his shoulders.

"You and Uncle Roman were asking my mom and dad about it," Dexter said as she steered him away from Cody and Demmy.

A dark chuckle snuck up on Cody, and he gave Roman a long, cool look. "Seems to be the question of the season. Rather than whether or not Dad's okay after spending a night somewhere out in the snow."

"Cody—"

"Shut your damn mouth, Roman." Cody's cool look turned into a glare. "So we can move on to more important items, I will answer Dexter's question." He took a breath and reached out to grab hold of Demmy's hand. "Yes, Demmy and I are in a romantic relationship."

"Hooray!" Dexter said. "I like Demetrius."

Demmy let out a long, slow breath and squeezed his hand. Cody smiled at him before looking around the silent kitchen. "Any questions?"

"I have so many questions," Roman said.

"Fire away."

"Roman, there are children in the house," Madison said in a creepy, sing-song voice, promptly moving Dexter out of the room.

"Dudes, why are you so torqued up about this?" Grant asked. He crossed the room and pulled Cody into a strong hug that left him with tears in his eyes. Then, he hugged Demmy and stood between them with an arm around each of their shoulders.

"This should be a celebration. We've known Dems since he was younger than Dexter. We love Dems, and we love Codes. Why can't we love them together?" Grant frowned. "Where did Madison take Dexter? He should be in here."

Grant left the kitchen. Before Cody could say anything, Dave practically ran across the kitchen to embrace him. When Dave finally let him go, Cody saw tears in Dave's eyes.

"I'm really happy for you, Cody."

"Thanks, man." He looked over at Demmy and was surprised to see Brady giving him a hug.

"This is really good news," Dave said. He had a wide smile that showed off his deep dimples. "You look happy and content."

"That's how I feel, so I'm glad it's coming through."

Brady and Dave switched places and Cody hugged his youngest brother.

"Proud of you," Brady said.

Cody frowned. "Proud? For what?"

"For being you."

"Well, thanks. Not sure that's a popular opinion right now."

"It is for me."

Brady and Dave moved out of the way as Cody's mother approached. She smiled and blinked back tears.

"You're happy?" she asked.

"I'm very happy."

"Then I'm happy for you."

She hugged Cody first, then Demmy. When she stepped back, she kept her hands on Demmy's shoulders and said, "Not really the holiday visit you expected, is it?"

Demmy laughed. "No, it's really not."

"I've got something that'll help. Come with me." She took him by the hand and led him out of the kitchen as Grant returned with Dexter, Brooke, and Conrad trailing behind him.

"Where are you two going?" Grant asked.

"To talk," she said. "Can you finish up the cocoa?"

As his mother led Demmy out of the kitchen, he looked back over his shoulder at Cody with wide eyes. Cody shrugged before Dexter practically tackled him with a hug around his thighs.

"Can I call Demetrius uncle now?" Dexter asked.

"If you want to," Cody said.

Brooke and Conrad stood just in front of Grant, both looking like they wished they were somewhere else.

"Do you have something to say to your uncle Cody?" Grant said.

"I don't know," Conrad mumbled with a half shrug and a flip of his hair.

"Congrats?" Brooke said, more of a question.

"Grant, you didn't have to bring your kids in here," Cody said.

"My feelings exactly," Roman said. Cody was glad Demmy wasn't around to hear him.

Before Cody could reply, Grant called into the living room, "Summer! Brock! You want to help with hot cocoa?"

Roman's kids appeared moments later, and Cody grinned. Despite Roman's assertive personality and tendency to run roughshod over other people, Grant was the oldest of them and always seemed to know when to step in and take charge.

"They were fine doing what they were doing," Roman said.

"We were just watching Rudolph," Brock said.

"Yeah, like, again," Summer said. "We can help with the cocoa."

"Do you want to give your uncle Cody a hug first?" Grant asked as he stirred the big pot of cocoa.

Summer frowned at Cody. "Why? Did something happen?"

"No," Roman snapped. His face was growing an alarming shade of red as he glared at Grant. "I do not tell you how to raise your children, Grant. And I expect—no, I demand, the same in return."

"Dad? What's wrong?" Brock asked.

Guilt churned within Cody's gut. He'd told them all about him and Demmy out of spite instead of celebration. He'd once more fired off at the mouth without first thinking about the consequences. He watched Roman practically push his kids out of the kitchen and stomp after them.

"Shit," he muttered.

"Uncle Cody said a bad word," Dexter said as he stood on tiptoes to try and see into the pan of cocoa.

"It's not that bad of a word," Conrad said. "They say it on TV now."

"Doesn't mean it's not a bad word," Grant said. He pulled a chair over and helped Dexter climb up. "Stir the cocoa just like this. Okay?"

"Okay." Dexter poked the tip of his tongue out of the side of his mouth.

Cody followed Grant out of the kitchen. He grabbed Grant's arm as he headed for the hallway.

"Grant, why not let it be for now? Let him cool down."

"He disrespected you and Dems in our parents' house. And hiding something like this from his kids because it makes him uncomfortable isn't right. It's not right at all."

"Yeah, I know that. But we've got bigger issues here. Dad's still missing, and we all need to be focused on supporting Mom right now. Okay?"

Grant slumped his shoulders. "You're right, Codes. He just really gets my hackles up."

"He's good at that." Cody looked around. "Where are Mom and Demmy?"

"Dunno. They put on boots and coats and went outside."

"Dad!" Brooke shouted from the kitchen.

"Coming!"

Cody stood in the living room and stared at the front door. He could hear Grant shushing the kids in the kitchen about the near miss on the cocoa boiling over, and from the end of the hall Roman and Madison talking with Summer and Brock. The urge to leave the house reared up within him, strong and nearly impossible to refuse.

Dave approached him with a steaming mug of cocoa in each hand. He handed one mug to Cody and clinked his against it.

"Cheers, big brother."

"Thanks."

Cody took a careful sip and blinked in surprise. "That's a really strong cup of cocoa."

"It's about a quarter peppermint schnapps."

"Have I ever told you that you're my favorite brother?"

Dave smiled. "Right back at you, Codes."

They laughed together before moving to the sofa and sitting at either end.

"So how did this thing develop between you and Demetrius?"

Cody shrugged and sipped again, savoring the heat and the booze. "I guess I just realized there was more between him and me than I'd always thought."

"Had you ever been with a guy before?"

"No. Came close a few times, though. There have definitely been guys I was attracted to, but I never acted on it."

"I have a few times."

Cody's mouth dropped open. "Really?"

Dave lifted one shoulder in a half shrug. "Yeah, sure. A couple of guys in college. And one guy I met through friends at a bar. We got really close as friends and were together for about two months, but things just didn't work out."

Cody slid closer and lowered his voice. "I never knew that. Why didn't you tell me?"

"And I direct that same question back to you."

"Yeah, all right. Fair enough." Cody sipped again. Whether it was the schnapps or the entire situation, he lowered his voice a little more and asked, "Did you do... everything with him?"

"Everything?"

"You know." Cody raised his eyebrows. "Everything."

Dave smirked. "I pitched and caught, if that's what you're asking."

The intensity of Cody's blush made him feel as if he'd dumped the cocoa directly down his throat. "And it was... okay?"

"Haven't you done it?"

"Well, one way."

"Just the one way?"

"It's complicated."

"It doesn't seem to be for Demetrius."

"Dammit, Dave."

Dave set his mug on the coffee table and leaned in closer, also lowering his voice. "Dude. You seriously have to try bottoming for him."

Cody put his face in his hands. "How did we get on this subject?"

"I blame the schnapps."

"I'm going to need the rest of the bottle to recover from this conversation."

"You'll be fine. And let me assure you, when he's sliding over that little nub inside you with a direct line to Heaven, you're going to thank me."

"All of this is making me feel very uncomfortable."

"Drink more of your cocoa."

Cody picked up his mug, surprised to find so little left. "How did I drink so much of this so fast?"

"I think it's called seeing your entire family for the holidays, and then telling them you're in a gay relationship."

"Yeah. But I haven't told everyone in the family yet."

Cody and Dave shared a sad smile.

"You think Dad's okay?" Dave asked.

"I do. I can't think otherwise because my brain just won't allow me to consider a world without him in it."

"I wonder where he is."

Cody looked toward the kitchen and the hallway, checking to make sure no one else was around before he pulled out his phone. He was about to show Dave the photos he took of the footprint and the fur on the side mirror support when Summer and Brock entered the living room from the hallway. Brock hurried into the kitchen where Cody heard him ask for some cocoa, but Summer hesitated and threw a nervous look at Cody.

Roman came up behind her and placed a hand flat against

her back. "Let's go, Summer. Get some cocoa and drink it in the kitchen."

He ignored Cody and Dave as he followed Summer out of the room. That brief interaction left Cody cold, and he no longer felt the urge to share the photos.

"Let me get you a refill." Dave stood and picked up both mugs. "Same mix okay?"

Cody held up his thumb and forefinger a short distance apart. "Maybe a wee bit more schnapps this time."

Dave grinned. "That's the Christmas spirit."

As Dave walked into the kitchen, Cody watched the front door. Where had his mom taken Demmy? Should he be worried? He ran his thumb up and down the glass of his phone, wondering if he should send Demmy a text.

Deciding against it for the moment, he slid the phone into his front pocket and slumped back into the couch. Family sucked. Well, most of his family. Okay, some of his family. However it worked out, Christmas was still two long days away.

CHAPTER NINE

Wind whipped snow into Demetrius's face, and he held a hand up in an effort to block the onslaught as he followed Cody's mother along the narrow, recently shoveled path toward the greenhouse. He had no idea what she had to say to him, but it would be a thousand times better than being back in the house with all of Cody's brothers and extended family members.

As stressful as the whole situation was, he felt proud of Cody for telling his family the truth about their relationship. He was nervous about interacting with all of them again, but he didn't really care. Cody had spoken up.

Alice entered a code on the lock's number pad, and then stepped inside the greenhouse. She held the door open for him, and once they were both inside and the door closed, she looked at him.

"That's always a fun trek in the winter. Summer is an entirely different story, but winter makes it tough sometimes to come out here."

They removed their coats and boots. When Demetrius

turned toward the cubbies where the slippers and coveralls waited, Alice stopped him with a hand on his forearm.

"No need for the protective wear. We're not going into the greenhouse itself."

"Oh, okay." Not sure what else to say, Demetrius added, "I'm really impressed with what Grant has setup out here."

"Yes, he really seems to have found his calling. Greg and I did a lot of research before we invested our money in this place. He's got some big plans, and Greg and I both make sure we keep tabs on what he does with the product."

"I don't think I've had the chance to tell you how sorry I am that Mr. Bower is missing."

She flashed a quick smile and turned away, but not before Demetrius saw her wipe away a tear. "Let's go into the office."

"There's an office?"

"Oh, it's not very big, just a place for one or two of us to meet and talk about things."

"How many people work in the greenhouse?"

"There's Greg and myself, and Grant, and his girlfriend Mac helps out on occasion, but she's usually busy teaching at the yoga studio. On occasion a young man from the Seed Share group helps out as well."

"Would that be Fleck?"

She looked surprised. "How do you know Fleck?"

"I don't, but Grant took a call from him when he was showing us around out here."

She nodded before leading him to a door she unlocked with a key she took from her coat pocket.

"We have to keep everything locked up," she said over her shoulder. "It's not just good business, but it's the law here in Colorado. Because there are minors living on the premises, everything has to be locked down." She waved a hand as she stepped into the small office and flicked on an overhead light.

"Grant knows all of this stuff inside and out. He did a lot of research before we decided to do all of this."

The office was claustrophobically small. A large desk took up a majority of the space, with a beaten up leather chair behind it and two straight-backed chairs in front. A number of Mason jars lined a shelf on the wall beside the desk. Each one had been secured with a lid, holding at least a dozen rolled joints. Labels written in black felt pen listed names like Granite Brainstorm, Blizzard Buzz, and Sweet Rock Climb.

Cody's mom took two joints out of a jar labeled High Altitude. "Do you smoke?"

Demetrius laughed nervously. "Um, no. Just once or twice in college."

"Would you like to smoke with me?"

"Oh, Mrs. Bower, you know—"

"Call me Alice. And you have to call Mr. Bower Greg. So when we find him, you make sure to call him that, all right?" Tears trembled on her lower eyelids, and Demetrius fought back his own.

"Of course." He couldn't really refuse her invitation after she'd led him out here away from the scene inside the house. He gave a single nod and held out a hand. "Okay, yeah. I'll join you. But this is very strange for me."

"I don't want to force you to do something you're not comfortable with," Alice said. "I can put this right back in the jar and sit outside to smoke."

"No. I'm—I'm okay with it." Even though he was nervous, Demetrius was intrigued and found himself looking forward to the experience. He had hoped his reacquaintance with pot would have been with Cody and not his mom, but this seemed important to her. And to him, if he was honest with himself. He really wanted to get to know Cody's mom as an adult. And a pot grower. She was practically running a small business out here with Grant and Mr.

Bower. Maybe she would have some tips about being a small business owner.

"Good. I hate to smoke alone."

He accepted the joint and they both sat in one of the straight-backed chairs. She flicked a silver lighter she had picked up from the desktop, and he leaned in to light the tip of the joint. Demetrius closed one eye against the smoke as he took his first drag, Alice watching him with a half smile.

"It has been a long time for you."

He nodded as he held the smoke, then broke into a coughing fit. Alice chuckled before taking a hit herself. They smoked in comfortable silence for a time, and soon Demetrius felt a warm sense of relaxation. His thoughts clicked together in succinctly formed rows, and he was able to pause the normally rapid flow of feelings and impressions and examine certain notions and thoughts more closely.

"It's my fault, you know," Alice said finally. "Greg being gone."

Demetrius shook his head before letting out his lungful of smoke, this time with no coughing. "Wasn't you. It was bigfoot."

Alice frowned. "Bigfoot? You mean sasquatch?"

He nodded as he took another hit. "I think it stepped out in front of his truck and he hit it. That's why he went off the road."

She looked at him, and then she held out her hand. "Maybe you've had enough. Give that back to me."

Demetrius grinned. "I haven't felt this good in… Hell, I've never felt like this. Grant grows some excellent pot."

"Product."

"You've got some grade A awesome product."

Alice's smile was shaky. She turned away and put her face in her hands, shoulders shaking with the force of her sobs.

"Oh, shit." Demetrius placed his joint in an ashtray on the

desk and leaned over to put an arm around her shoulders. "Mrs. Bower… sorry, Alice. Come on, we'll find Mr. Bower. Damn. We'll find Greg. It's going to be all right. Don't cry."

"It won't be all right," Alice said as she sat up and wiped away tears. "He's been out there for almost two full nights now. If he hasn't frozen to death, he soon will. And he wouldn't have been out there if it wasn't for me."

"I'm sure that's not true. You two have been together for a really long time. Cody and I used to say we felt left out in high school and college because all our other friends' parents were divorced and ours were still together."

She flashed a trembling smile and put her hands on her thighs, fingers curled into fists. "We argued yesterday. I pushed him to do something before the boys arrived, and he didn't want to do it again. But I didn't listen, like usual. This time he just walked out. He grabbed his keys and left without saying a word."

"I've made mistakes," Alice said with a slow shake of her head. "So many of them. But I came from a large family who had nothing to call our own. My father bounced around from job to job, and my mother did what she could for the nine of us, but it never seemed to be enough."

"Nine kids?"

She nodded. "Nine. Can you imagine?"

"No. I don't know how you managed to raise five boys."

Alice laughed. "Sometimes I don't either. Greg helped a lot, I have to give him credit for that."

She looked so sad, Demetrius wished he could say or do something to make her smile. But his thoughts were inching along at a snail's pace, and his decision-making seemed to have shut down. He couldn't decide if he wanted to hug her or pat her shoulder or just smile and nod with understanding. So he just settled on staring as she kept talking.

"Greg's always been my strength, you know? He sees

something in me that I have never been able to. He believes in me so much, and I keep turning my back on him."

Some words of comfort floated to the top of his mind. "I'm sure that's not true."

"It is. And it's worse than anyone else knows." She wiped away more tears. "Well, Grant knows. But none of his brothers."

A dark and disturbing line of thought oozed out of the slow parade of contemplations. Before he could stop himself, Demetrius asked, "Did you murder Mr. Bower?"

Alice's wide-eyed reaction gave him the answer before she even opened her mouth. "What? No! I would never harm Greg. I love him with all of my heart, and it's taken this tragedy to make me clearly see what I might have lost."

Sweet relief pulsed through Demetrius. He should be asking follow-up questions, but first he needed to figure out what they were. The word "tragedy" pinged about his brain, and he frowned as he considered it.

"Is it?" he asked.

"Is what it?"

"A tragedy."

"My husband drove off the road and is missing. I would call that a tragedy."

"I guess. A tragedy to me would be if he had been killed in the accident, and we'd found his body. Or if bigfoot had pulled him from the truck and dismembered him there on the spot. I would consider that a tragedy. But since he's only missing and not dead, I don't know if I'd go so far as to call it a tragedy."

Alice blinked. "You are way too high for your own good, aren't you?"

Demetrius grinned. "I have never been this relaxed."

"Oh dear. Cody is going to kill me."

"Nah. He's a big, huggable sweetheart. He loves me, you know."

"He's told you that?" Alice's smile was contagious.

"Once. When he was about to be carried off by a swamp monster."

She frowned, wrinkling her forehead, and it looked like the most amazing topographic map Demetrius had ever seen.

"Swamp monster?" Alice slid the ashtray where the two half joints rested out of Demetrius's reach. "You seem to be fixated on monster legends. Have you always liked them?"

"Legends is one word for them. Brutally real is another. Wait, that's two words."

"Have you seen a sasquatch? And a swamp monster?"

"Yes. No, wait. No. Well, maybe on a sasquatch, but yes to a swamp monster."

"Where did you see the sasquatch? You said something a little while ago that it may have caused Greg's accident. Were you serious?"

"We don't know for sure, you know? But we're pretty good at figuring these things out, and we've found some stuff."

"What kind of stuff?"

"A giant footprint. And fur." He giggled. "Footprints and Fur. Sounds like the title for a gay werewolf love triangle series." His eyes went wide and he pointed at Alice. "No! A gay sasquatch love triangle series."

"Demetrius, think."

He scrunched up his face. "You're right. It would have to be werewolves. They're more popular."

"No. Think back on what you found about Greg's accident."

"There's nothing left. The plows got rid of the prints, and the truck's at the police yard for now." A yawn snuck up on him, and he slouched down. "I like that stuff. What do you call it?"

"High Altitude."

"That I am. I feel like I could sleep for a year. How about you?"

Alice nodded, but Demetrius didn't think she was really listening to him any longer. He pushed himself up in the chair. "You're thinking some heavy stuff."

"I'm concerned about Greg. I thought he might have staged the accident and run off, but what you're saying makes me think otherwise."

"Staged the accident? Why would he do that?"

"Because he was angry and hurt about something I did. Something I've been doing."

Demetrius looked at the joints in the ashtray. Alice was bringing him down with her emotional talk, but he didn't think he should smoke any more. And the pot had him feeling horny, too. His cock was half-hard and eager to get up to full mast.

Maybe Cody's dad was upset they were growing pot.

"Is it because of the pot?" Demetrius whispered.

"Oh, no. It was mainly his idea to help Grant with the greenhouse. After they showed me the research about benefits of cannabis, I couldn't say no." She shrugged. "I haven't slept so soundly or been this relaxed in years. Maybe ever. No, he wasn't upset about the pot; Greg was upset about the swinging."

Demetrius frowned. "Swinging? Is he afraid of heights?"

Alice tipped her head back and let out a loud, tinkling laugh that made Demetrius smile. He was so glad he'd made her laugh that way. Now he could rest easy knowing he'd given her a little bit of joy. But he was still confused about why Cody's dad didn't like swings.

"Oh you sweet boy. I can see why Cody has fallen for you."

"My masculine good looks?"

She smiled. "Of course." Then she moved a little closer and lowered her voice. "Greg and I have had some disagreements about entertaining other couples. In the bedroom. You know what I mean?"

"Mom?"

Cody's voice made them both jump. Demetrius tried hard to grasp the fact that Cody's mother had just told him she and Cody's father had sex with other couples. He felt guilty, as if he'd been caught doing something truly awful with Cody's mother, and he got to his feet. But he had nowhere to go when Cody stepped inside the office.

"Hi!" Demetrius said, his voice much too loud and too high-pitched even to his own ears.

Cody grinned. "Hi yourself." He looked around Demetrius to his mother. "And how are the two of you doing?"

"Oh, we're fine. Aren't we, Demetrius?"

"What? Yes. Fine. We're fine. How are you?"

"Well, I'm pretty tired, actually. And I want to get up early and join the search from the beginning, so I was thinking of going to bed."

"Okay. Yep. I'm ready. Let's go to bed." Demetrius stopped and looked between Cody and Alice as he blushed. "I mean. Let's go to Grant's apartment and get into our separate sleeping bags."

Alice smiled and hugged Demetrius. "Welcome to the family. I've always loved you like a sixth son." She pulled back and frowned at him. "That came out sounding much ickier than I intended, now that the two of you are bumping uglies."

"Mom!"

Demetrius's high-pitched cackle was unexpected and completely involuntary.

"What?" Alice still gripped Demetrius's upper arms, and she looked around him at Cody. "Isn't that what kids these days call having sex?"

"If by 'these days' you mean the seventies, then yes, that's what they're calling it."

Alice released Demetrius, who watched with a stunned smile as Cody leaned down to give her a hug.

"You okay, Mom?" Cody asked, the concern evident in his voice.

"I'm doing all right. Demetrius helped me feel better."

"Yeah. And you apparently helped him feel better, too."

"He had half a joint. Just enough to help him relax after that scene back at the house." She took one of their hands in each of her own and looked between them. "I don't care who you sleep with or who you fall in love with, as long as you're respectful, careful, and happy."

"Well, I can say yes to all of those things," Cody said.

"Me, too," Demetrius added.

"Good. Now, go get some rest. We'll have another long day tomorrow."

Demetrius looked at Cody as Alice slipped out of the office. Cody stood with his arms crossed and a big grin on his amazingly handsome face as he looked right back at him.

"You got high with my mom."

"What? No. You did."

"You are really high right now."

"Shut up. You're high."

"I bet you've got the munchies like nobody's business, don't you?"

"No."

"Liar."

"A liar that you love."

Cody's grin settled into a more seductive smirk. "You're right. I do love you."

Demetrius didn't know what to think or say. His thoughts, once lined up in one neat, slow-moving train, seemed to have derailed. All he could do was repeat the words back to him. "You love me."

The sound of Alice leaving the greenhouse echoed through the office space and Cody stepped closer. "I do. I love you, Demmy."

"I love you, too."

"I had a feeling you might."

"What gave it away?"

Cody palmed the bulge in his pants. "This interesting reaction that happens when I'm around you."

The kiss that followed sent fireworks popping and exploding around Demetrius's mind. All thought had stopped when Cody said he loved him, but now the very existence of thought vanished. He had no concept of thinking or breathing or life outside of the kiss. It was his everything, and he let himself be swept up by the touch of Cody's tongue, the feel of Cody's big hand on the back of his head, and the heat from Cody's body engulfing him.

When Cody finally broke the embrace, he pulled back and stared at Demetrius, his pupils big and his swollen lips parted.

"What the fuck did you smoke with my mom?"

Demetrius waved a hand in the general direction of the table. "That. She called it High Altitude."

"We need to get some of that back home."

Demetrius groped Cody's cock and balls through his pants. "I want you."

Cody closed the office door. He picked Demetrius up and sat him on the edge of the desk then pushed the chairs out of his way. He kissed Demetrius hard and struggled with the button and zipper on Demetrius's pants until he'd freed him. Demetrius leaned back and braced himself on the desk as Cody went down on him. He closed his eyes and dropped his head back, surrendering himself to Cody's mouth and tongue. Colors burst and spiraled on the insides of his eyelids as he seemed to float in a dark warm space. Each suck and lick pushed him deeper into this space, and he gasped and lifted his hips, thrusting to meet Cody's mouth as it came down. Cody moaned around him, and the vibration was enough to tip him over the edge. The pulses of his orgasm sent waves of color washing through him as Cody swallowed every drop Demetrius gave him.

"Fuck, that was hot," Cody said, running his tongue up his length and taking him to the root once more.

Demetrius shivered, hands clenched into fists against the desktop, the buttons of his shirt undone as Cody ran a hand up and down his chest, the hair threading through his fingers. Cody stood and grabbed each side of Demetrius's open shirt to pull him upright in order to plant a hard kiss on his mouth. Demetrius tasted himself on Cody's tongue, and he thought it was the most intimate and sexy thing he'd ever experienced.

"I want you," Demetrius said around tongue-heavy and sloppy kisses. "I need to taste you, too."

"Oh no, not that," Cody said in mock disapproval.

In moments, Cody had his pants open and Demetrius took hold of him. His dick pulsed hard and hot against his palm as he stroked and continued kissing Cody. They awkwardly shifted position, both shuffling because their pants were around their ankles, and they laughed in the middle of a kiss. Cody held Demetrius's face between his palms and his expression was so calm and loving, it stopped Demetrius's breath.

"God, I love you, Demmy."

Demetrius had been mulling over those wonderful,

dangerous words for weeks now. Only Cody had said them first, and more perfectly than Demetrius could have ever managed.

"I love you, too."

"I don't know how you put up with me."

Demetrius kissed him and gently pushed him back until he sat on the edge of the desk. "We put up with each other because we know there's no one better for us out there." He unbuttoned Cody's shirt and spread it open, then placed a gentle kiss in the center of his chest, feeling the tickle of the patch of hair that grew there.

Cody moved in for another kiss. "You've got that right."

With a hand on the center of Cody's chest, Demetrius pushed him back so he sat on the desk. Cody's heart beat fast, and Demetrius imagined he could feel it swell with love. Pulling up a chair, Demetrius sat between Cody's legs and leaned forward to take him in his mouth. He kept one hand against Cody's chest, feeling his heart pound faster as he stroked and sucked him. Every few pumps, he stopped to run his tongue around the fat head and give it a hard suck.

Demetrius closed his eyes, reveling in the experience. He loved sucking Cody, loved the feel of his hard length along his tongue, tasting the bitter pre-cum, the pulse of his shaft as he gripped Cody tight.

Moments later, Cody groaned and thrust his hips up as Demetrius descended. Demetrius waited for his quiet hitching gasp, and then he plunged his mouth down, taking him deep into his throat as Cody erupted in his mouth. Demetrius swallowed it all down, savoring the briny taste he had come to know so well.

He slowly pulled back and left a gentle kiss on the very tip of Cody's dick before he sat back. Cody looked worn out, his eyes half-closed and his cheeks flushed pink. His lips were still swollen from kissing and sucking, and they glistened in the glow of the overhead light.

"We are definitely finding a way to get some of that pot back home," Cody said.

Demetrius laughed and tipped the chair back on two legs as he waved his arms overhead. He'd never felt so free and so alive. Colorado was amazing.

CHAPTER TEN

Cody grinned as he watched Demmy try to work the zipper of his coat.

"Seriously?" Cody finally said.

Demmy looked up, eyes glassy. "What?"

"Come here." Cody moved in close, zipped Demmy's coat up for him, and then leaned in for a kiss. "You're really fucking hot when you're stoned."

"You're really fucking hot all the time."

"Dude. We should have gotten a hotel room."

Demmy frowned. "How come?"

"So I could fuck you long and deep right now. You've got me really turned on."

Demmy cupped his crotch. "Really?"

"Let's go before I make a huge mess in here." Cody started for the door, then stopped and walked quickly back to the office.

"This is the exit," Demmy called to his back.

"Give me a minute." In the office, Cody opened the container marked High Altitude and selected two precisely rolled joints. He hesitated, then plucked out two more.

Stashing them in his coat pocket, he secured the container lid and returned to where Demmy waited by the exit.

"Forget something?"

"Kind of. Let's go."

The wind pushed against them as they made their way toward the garage. Cody squinted through the snow and saw the lights on in Grant's apartment. He hoped no one was home because he really wanted to make out with Demmy while he was still so relaxed. If marijuana legalization ever hit the ballots in Pennsylvania, he was definitely voting for it.

They were both winded by the time they had climbed the steps and got inside, and they sat for a moment on the bench in the mudroom to catch their breath. The bench was small, and Cody's thigh and hip pressed against Demmy's. Even after having sex with Demmy for the last few months, simple moments of connection like this sometimes really affected him. He smiled and put a hand on Demmy's thigh.

"I know this hasn't been an easy trip."

Demmy shrugged. "It's not your fault."

"Still, I wanted you to know that I'm sorry, and I'll try to make it better for you."

"It's not about me or you. It's about finding your dad, and that's how it should be right now. Tomorrow we'll join the search and hopefully find some sign of him." Demmy put his hand over Cody's and squeezed. "I'm here for you, however you need me to be."

Cody grinned. "You just helped me out a lot in the greenhouse."

"We helped each other out."

After a quick kiss, they removed their outer wear and stepped into the kitchen. Cody was headed for the refrigerator when Demmy grabbed his wrist.

"What?"

Demmy stared into the living room. "Do you see that?"

Cody stood behind Demmy and looked over his head. Mac was in a yoga pose in the living room, arms stretching toward the ceiling, shaved head tipped back and eyes closed.

"Yeah, it's Mac. Let's give her a few minutes."

"You can come in and sit down," Mac said. She retained her pose and her lips barely moved, making Cody wonder if she'd spoken to him telepathically.

"We'll give you some space," Cody said.

"I'm almost done."

"Okay." Demmy wandered into the living room and dropped onto one of the sofas.

Cody stood where he was a moment, and then sat beside Demmy. They faced Mac on her yoga mat, and he couldn't help thinking it felt like she was performing some kind of living art exhibit. He hated those things.

"I'm making you uncomfortable," Mac said as she switched poses but still didn't look at them.

"What? No. Not at all." Cody let out a fake yawn. "We're just tired. Been a long day."

"Yes. For everyone. Greg's disappearance has stressed the usual polite bonds within the family, and now there's blood in the water." Mac had her head down and her ass in the air, and still she didn't make eye contact.

"Plus it's Christmas," Demmy added. "And that can really stress people out."

Mac grinned. "The holidays are practically designed for that."

Demmy yawned and leaned his head against Cody's shoulder.

"I'm glad you came out to your family." Mac stood up and lifted her hands to the ceiling, her movements slow and fluid.

Cody snorted quietly. "Yeah, tell that to Roman."

"Roman claims to worship God, but his religion is money. His wife is the same way, but his children are surprisingly open to new people and experiences." She lowered herself into a cross-legged position in one smooth movement and pressed her palms together in front of her. Cody heard her whisper, "Namaste," before she finally made eye contact and smiled. "They are very different from you. I was curious how you would react to the changes your family has gone through."

"You talking about Hemp House or something else?"

Mac smiled as she rose to her feet. The low lamp-light gleamed across her scalp and the wind batted ice crystals against the window glass.

"All of it. You've handled Hemp House well. You'll manage the rest."

Demmy snored quietly against Cody's shoulder while a nervous energy coiled low in his belly. What more could he have to learn about his family?

"What do you mean?"

Mac got on her knees to roll up the yoga mat. "You'll find out soon enough. Don't worry, there's no crime involved."

"Well, that's a fucking relief."

She smiled and silently left the room. Cody wanted to get up and follow, but Demmy lay sleeping peacefully against him. And, when he thought about it, he wasn't sure he was ready to find out what she meant. He had a lot on his plate to process. First and foremost was finding his father. Second was understanding what those marijuana plants meant to his brother and parents. Were they all smoking and eating it? For what purposes, other than the obvious? And third was dealing with Roman and his family.

But for now, Cody was content to sit on the couch, Demmy sleeping on his shoulder and the wind whipping around the apartment. Despite the harsh weather conditions, Cody found a stubborn nugget of hope that his father was still alive. Maybe he had been found by some remote farmer whose phone lines had come down in the snow and who had no mobile phone. Or he'd found a shallow cave or rocky overhang and built a fire. Or maybe even a small hunting cabin, closed for the winter, that provided shelter and a few canned goods. Perhaps some kind soul outside of town had found him wandering and confused and taken him in, or to a hospital.

Cody made a mental note to ask his mother if she had checked the local hospitals. He was sure the police had done that, but he wanted to make sure his mom had heard the results.

Demmy shifted in his sleep and Cody took the opportunity to slip out from beneath him and gently lower him to the cushions. He put Demmy's feet up on the couch and covered him with a warm quilt that looked handmade. After a stop in the hallway bathroom, Cody listened for any sounds of Mac. All was dark and quiet at the far end of the hallway, back where the bedrooms were situated. Apparently, Mac went to bed early. Unless it was really late. He checked his phone display and was surprised to discover it was 9:30. Mountain time really messed him up.

The apartment was quiet except for the wind whistling around the corners and Demmy's deep, soft breathing. Though he'd been exhausted when he'd left the house looking for Demmy, he now wasn't tired enough to just give up and go to sleep. But he also didn't feel like spending time with his family. Some time on his own would be nice, allow him to collect his thoughts and maybe come up with a new plan to find his father.

He opened drawers in the kitchen until he found the standard catch-all. A collection of pens and a few notepads lay mixed in with household tools, coupons, and Chip Clips. He wrote a quick note and left it on the floor by the couch, weighted down by Demmy's phone. After pulling on boots, coat, hat, and gloves, he left the apartment.

Icy pellets of snow stung his cheeks and chin, and he held up a hand to block the assault as he made his way down the steps. The lights were on in the kitchen of the main house, but Cody turned toward the side door leading into the garage. It was unlocked, and he stepped inside and leaned back against the door, wiping melted snow from his face. Three cars could fit inside, with room left over for yard maintenance equipment or outdoor furniture. A smaller crossover vehicle, most likely his mother's, took up the nearest spot while Grant's big SUV was in the middle space.

Feeling very warm, Cody unzipped his coat and removed his hat and gloves. He realized the garage was heated and wondered how much it cost to winterize and heat that space. He considered the idea of doing the same to Amelia's single car garage back in Parson's Hollow, then laughed at himself. They couldn't fit either of their trucks inside the garage, so why would he bother?

He stuffed his gloves and hat into the pockets of his coat, then stopped when he touched the joints he'd taken from the office. While he wished Demmy were with him to share the experience, he really needed to relax. Now he just had to find a lighter.

He searched the workbench in the back corner, finding several cheap plastic lighters before he settled on a red one. After pulling a tarp off a well-cushioned lawn chair, Cody sat down and lit up. He took a few shallow puffs, then a longer, deeper drag he held for a long time. His toes started to relax, and then his feet. The feeling of looseness in his muscles climbed up his legs and into his chest. He took another deep hit then put his head back and closed his eyes. This was some really great stuff. His brother knew what he was doing out in the greenhouse.

When he'd pulled the tarp off the patio chair, he'd exposed the corners of several boxes stacked in the other patio chairs. His feet felt like they were made of stone, but his curiosity was piqued. He pinched the tip of the joint out and set it on the edge of the patio table, then got up and pulled away the tarp. Christmas gifts for the kids had been stacked in the chairs, and he squatted and ran his fingers over each box as he read the name.

A microscope, a telescope, a drone with an HD video camera, several board games, and some boxes that most likely contained articles of clothing. He wondered if something in the pile was for him and Demmy then quietly admonished himself for being selfish. He pulled the tarp back over everything, then remembered the joint and had to crawl around on the floor for a bit before he found it. His phone buzzed while he knelt on the warm concrete floor. It was a text from Demmy: *Where are you?*

He wrote back: *In the garage right below you.*

You alone?

Far as I know.

I'll come join you.

Cody pulled the tarp off the furniture and moved some of the gifts from one of the other chairs so Demmy would have a place to sit. Just as he sat down again, the side door opened and Demmy stepped inside, bundled up and covered with snow.

"Welcome to the warmest garage in history."

Demmy pulled off his gloves and hat and smiled. "It's warmer than my apartment."

"You mean your old apartment. We live together now, remember?"

"Yeah, I remember." Demmy slid off his coat and stepped out of his wet boots. "Wow, even the floor is heated."

"I know!" Cody waved to the chair beside him. "Have a

seat." He held up the remaining half of the joint. "Care for a little more High Altitude?"

"Maybe a hit or two, sure." Demmy sank into the chair. "This chair is really comfortable. Is this their patio furniture?"

"Better than my couch, right?"

"A lot better."

"Hey now, you don't have to be mean about it." Cody lit the joint and took a drag before handing it off to Demmy. "So how was your nap?"

"I feel like I slept the entire night." Demmy hit the joint and passed it back. "What time is it?"

Cody checked his phone. "Ten thirty."

"That's it?" He shook his head. "Mountain time."

"That's what I thought, too."

Demmy spotted the gifts piled up in the other chairs. "Are those Christmas gifts?" He grinned. "Did you uncover Santa's stash?"

"Leave it to me to ruin a surprise." He passed the joint back. "Did I ever tell you how I found out there's no Santa?"

"No. Tell me."

"I was helping my parents load the car with Christmas gifts and luggage to go to my grandparents' house, and I found the roll of Santa paper. They were stone cold busted."

Demmy frowned as he held his breath, then as the smoke trickled out, asked, "Santa paper?"

"Yeah. The gifts from Santa were always wrapped in the same paper. Didn't your parents do that?"

"I don't really remember. Dad would pass out the gifts, and it all became a blur."

"Yeah, you always got a shit ton of gifts. Lucky only child."

Demmy shrugged and declined when Cody held the joint out again. "I'm good." He closed his eyes and folded his hands over his stomach. "I don't remember how I learned there was no Santa. Maybe some kids at school told me or something." He opened his eyes. "I don't remember you trying to tell me about it. Why didn't we talk about it?"

"I didn't know if you still believed or not. And I had just spent Christmas with my family at my grandparents' house. I was probably triple traumatized by the time I got home and could barely talk."

"I have never known you to be barely able to talk."

"Are you suggesting I'm too chatty?"

"I would be surprised if you were unable to talk. That's all I'm saying."

"Sounds like you think I talk too much."

"You're kind of proving my point right now."

"It's this pot. It does something to you."

"Yeah, it relaxes you, if you let it."

Cody finished off the joint then stretched out his legs and slouched in the chair. He studied Demmy's profile and realized he was incredibly horny again. He had to admit, he was a High Altitude fan. Maybe instead of giving people the munchies, High Altitude got them relaxed and horny. It was a nice trade off.

"How's it feel the second time around?" Cody asked.

Demmy opened one eye. "Pretty much the same. How's it feel for you?"

"I'm feeling a little worked up, if you know what I mean."

"I always know what you mean." Demmy looked around. "No windows in here?"

"Nope."

"Does the door lock?"

Cody was out of his chair and across the garage in a flash as Demmy laughed. Once he'd twisted the thumb lock in the knob, Cody turned off a couple banks of lights to set a more intimate mood before standing in front of Demmy's chair.

"Look at that package." Demmy ran a hand up and down

the fattening bulge in Cody's jeans. "I'm going to be surprised on Christmas morning."

"You've been good this year. You can open your present early."

"Really?" Demmy unbuttoned Cody's jeans and slowly lowered the zipper. "I don't like to rip the paper. It's such a pretty package."

Demmy lifted the waistband of Cody's briefs out and down to release his cock and caught the tip of it on his tongue. He sucked him deep into his throat, and Cody groaned.

"Feels so good." Cody pushed his pants and underwear down and stepped out of them, then peeled off his thermal shirt so he was just wearing his socks. "I love your mouth."

"I love you," Demmy said as he came up for a breath.

Cody leaned down to kiss him, and then he tugged Demmy out of the chair. They kissed as Cody pulled off Demmy's clothes piece by piece until he was down to his socks as well. Cody took the hard nub of a nipple between his teeth. Demmy took both of their cocks in hand and stroked. He squeezed out pre-cum and coated each of them with their mixed fluid.

"I love you," Cody said as he moved to Demmy's other nipple. "I can't seem to stop saying that."

"I feel the same way. But, I also feel like I need more than a blowjob."

That got Cody's immediate attention, and he straightened up to give Demmy a long serious look. "We don't have lube."

"Let's see what's out here."

Demmy lifted more tarps, his hard-on bobbing and weaving with each step. Cody smirked before looking beneath others. He found a chaise lounger with a thick pad and unfolded a beach towel to lay over it. When he turned he found Demmy grinning as he held up a small jar of petroleum jelly.

"The original lube." He removed the lid and used a couple of fingers to scoop out a generous helping. "Sit down."

Cody sat on the towel covering the chaise lounge, feet to either side and his cock standing up like a flagpole. Demmy approached and reached behind him to slide some jelly into himself before he coated Cody's dick with it. His slick grip felt so good Cody thought he might come just from Demmy's touch. Demmy straddled the chaise and slowly lowered himself onto Cody's cock.

"Fuck, Demmy, you are so fucking hot."

They shared a hard, hot kiss before Demmy began to move. With his feet planted on the concrete, Demmy rode Cody's dick hard and fast. A flutter started in Cody's chest and swiftly spread to his limbs. It was different from when his orgasm was closing in on him. This feeling was stronger, more intense. He gasped, his heart pounding.

Then Demmy moaned and Cody felt the hot splash of cum up his torso. Cody lifted his hips to meet Demmy as he descended, pushing a grunt out of him with each thrust. The loving feeling inside Cody's chest exploded into orgasm, and he thrust up a final time, lifting his ass off the chaise. He supported Demmy's full weight as Demmy balanced himself with his toes and a hand on Cody's shoulder. When he finished, Cody lowered himself to the chaise and, still inside Demmy, pulled him down for a kiss.

Sounds from outside the garage startled them, and when the knob rattled they pulled apart quickly, giggling quietly as they gathered their discarded clothes. Cody heard Grant's voice outside the door: "Someone must have locked the door. I gotta find the key in the drawer upstairs."

"Who would have locked the goddamn door?" Roman, right on the edge of anger as usual.

"Don't know, Romes. Lots of new peeps with free reign around the grounds this week."

"I gotta get my kids' gifts so Madison can wrap them. When am I supposed to do that?"

"Let me go look for the key, and I'll text you when the door's open. Just relax, Romes. It'll be okay."

Roman's heavy sigh came through the door loud and clear, and a petulant sense of satisfaction made Cody smirk.

"Fine," Roman said. "And stop calling me Romes."

They heard Grant go upstairs to his apartment and the crunch of snow as Roman stalked off. Demmy was dressed and had his hand over his mouth to keep from laughing. Cody pulled him close for a quick kiss, then checked to make sure they'd covered the outdoor items like they had found them. Demmy smoothed over the surface of the petroleum jelly and replaced the jar, then both of them put on boots, coats, hats, and gloves.

"Let's walk around the greenhouse once before going upstairs," Cody whispered.

Demmy nodded. "Good idea."

With a final, lingering kiss, Cody unlocked the door, opened it, and set the lock again before they slipped out into the snow.

CHAPTER ELEVEN

Sunlight gleamed across the fresh snowfall, and even though he wore sunglasses, Demetrius had to shade his eyes as he scanned the wide open field. To either side of him, volunteers high-stepped through the snow, each wearing a bright orange vest. Some carried long poles they used to poke into deep snow drifts and tree deadfalls.

"Break time already?" Brady, the youngest of the Bower men, chuckled as he passed Demetrius. "This high altitude can really get to you older folks."

Demetrius grinned and hurried to catch up with Brady. "I'm only five years older than you."

"Looks like those might have been a rough five years."

He had to give Brady some points on that observation. Hell, in the past year alone Demetrius felt like he'd aged ten years, what with the monster cases they'd worked.

"Yeah, yeah," Demetrius said. "Just keep your eyes open."

They were quiet for a time as they moved across the field in line with the other volunteers.

"Did you always love my brother?"

The question caught Demetrius off-guard and caused him

to falter a bit through his next two steps. But he regained his footing and composure as he kept aligned with Brady.

"It's kind of hard to explain," Demetrius started, unsure of what he was going to say next. No one had asked him about his feelings for Cody since they'd come out back home. He figured everyone had assumed they'd been having sex all along anyway. But Brady had moved away right after graduating high school, and now he lived in Louisiana. There had been just enough years between Brady and Cody to keep them away from each other's friends.

"Is it?" Brady glanced over and Demetrius might have caught a touch of sarcasm in his tone and expression. "You two hung out all the time growing up. Did you know you were gay all those years?"

"I didn't come out until high school," Demetrius said. "But I had known I was different since elementary school."

"And did my brother know?"

"He was one of the first people I came out to."

"Oh. That's interesting."

Brady fell silent, and Demetrius considered the word "interesting" until he finally asked, "What's interesting?"

"Just seems maybe you were fishing."

Demetrius knew where Brady was headed with his line of questioning, but he wanted him to say it outright, so he simply said, "Fishing?"

"Yeah." Brady gave him a quick look, and to his credit it appeared he might have been blushing. Or maybe it was just windburn. "Like you told him first to see if he might be interested."

Demetrius stopped walking, and it must have taken Brady a couple of steps to realize he wasn't alongside any longer. Brady walked back as the rest of the search volunteers continued across the field, headed toward a stand of trees.

"I don't mean to be offensive."

"But you are." Demetrius's tone shocked even himself. He hadn't realized just how upset he was until he'd started to speak. "You're suggesting I tried to manipulate my best friend into a relationship. From what you said, the fact that I trusted Cody more than any other person in my life and approached him with my biggest secret, means that rather than be honest with him, I simply wanted to try and get him to sleep with me out of some sense of pity or something." Demetrius looked away as he gathered his patience, picking out the back of Cody's head in the line of volunteers moving away from them at a steady pace.

"Demetrius—"

"No, you've talked enough. It's still my turn." He took a breath and looked back at Brady. "I'm not angry with you, Brady. I think you've been talking to Roman about this, and he's colored your opinion. It's your right to talk about your brother's decisions and question someone who's taken up a special place in his life. But the fact that you don't often call or email or text Cody and share any details of your own life does make me suspicious about your own intentions with this conversation. Or maybe you didn't think I would call you out on what you were saying, hoping I would be silent and accept your judgment and possibly break things off with Cody. Well, you can snuff that flicker of hope out right now. I've known your brother about as long as you've been alive, and I'm permanent, so you might as well get used to seeing me at holidays and hearing my voice in the background if you ever decide to call. What's between Cody and me isn't a phase, and it isn't just for fun. It's taken us over twenty years to get to this place, and I don't see it fading anytime soon."

Demetrius grew angrier as he vented and even more so when he found himself on the edge of tears. Dammit, why did he have to cry when he got angry?

"Wow. Okay. Can I speak now?"

He held up a gloved finger. "Not yet. I have one more thing to say to you. You're married to your high school girl-friend, Hilari. And you're going to have a baby soon. How long did you know you wanted to marry her? And how did you first ask her out? Think about your own experiences with your first true love and think about it from my point of view. It's not so different, you know. It's the same emotions with a hell of a lot more challenges."

He took a deep breath that plumed between them as he slowly released it. Back when they'd been kids, he and Cody had traded off pretending to be Godzilla in the winter, breathing fire on each other as they engaged in epic monster battles. Demetrius had loved the warm, moist touch of Cody's breath as it washed over him, but at that age he hadn't really understood why. Now he wished he could really breathe fire so he could sear Brady's face from his skull. But that wouldn't be the mature thing to do. So, he crossed his arms over his chest and held himself tight. His muscles trembled, from the cold or the height of his emotions he wasn't certain, but he gave Brady a single nod for him to speak.

"First off, I apologize," Brady said.

Demetrius relaxed somewhat, and his shoulders dropped a bit. "Okay. Accepted."

"You're right, I did talk with Roman about this. Or, rather, Roman talked at me about you and Cody. He's conservative, which you know, and he and Cody have always butted heads, which I'm sure you know as well."

"Yeah, I know." Cody and Roman had argued often while living under the same roof, and now they simply avoided all communication until they were forced to see each other at family gatherings. "They're very different."

"That's putting it mildly. But Roman brought up some good questions, and I thought it would be better coming from me."

"So you're his informant now?" Demetrius couldn't help the edge to his voice.

"I wouldn't say that. I think I'm more like a liaison."

"A liaison is along the same lines as a messenger. Just remember what they say about messengers."

Brady gave a nod. "I can see I've really upset you, and I didn't mean to. I was just looking out for Cody, so I hope you can understand my questions come from a place with good intentions for my brother."

"I get it. But I've been a part of many of your family gatherings almost all of your life, so you should understand why I'm offended at the conversation. You were questioning my motives for coming out to Cody. And not only is my coming out a very personal and private decision, as well as something you could never understand, but I would hope after all of these years you would see me as a trusted member of your extended family."

"You've made a lot of good points," Brady said, extending a hand. "Please know that I never meant to make any insinuations about your motives. I promise to keep more of a clear head when talking with Roman."

Demetrius shook with him. "I'm glad to hear that. You and Hilari live in Louisiana, and Roman and his family live in Utah. Do you see each other very often?"

"We Skype every other weekend."

"I see. I'm glad you keep in touch with him. Maybe you could extend that courtesy to Cody as well."

"I would like to keep in better touch with all of my brothers, especially now that we're expecting our first child."

"It's never too late to start something like that." Demetrius felt satisfied with where they were leaving things and looked around for the rest of the volunteers. No one was in sight, and a small quiver of nervousness went through him. Surely

Brady hadn't kept him talking so long to intentionally separate him from the group?

"We've lost everyone else," Brady said, sounding convincingly nervous.

"Let's head toward those trees," Demetrius suggested. "We'll be able to follow their tracks in the snow."

"I'm glad we've got plenty of daylight left," Brady said as they started walking.

"Oh, yeah, we'll be fine. We just need to catch up with the rest of the group."

They walked in silence to the first of the trees where they paused. A small amount of sunlight managed to sneak between the bare branches of the hardwood trees, but the snow-covered pines blocked much of the light. Demetrius could see the tracks of the group as they'd moved between the trunks and low-hanging branches of the trees, but he didn't see a single volunteer. How long had he and Brady had been talking?

"I didn't think they were walking that fast," Brady said in a low voice.

"Me either. But they can't be too far ahead of us, right?"

"Right. Yeah, sure."

"Let's go catch up."

They set out along separate trails through the snow, weaving around trees and bushes. Demetrius lost sight of Brady every now and then, but only for a few moments as a tree or two came between them. A prickly sense of anxiety gathered in the pit of Demetrius's stomach, and it kept him from calling out for Cody. Brady must have felt something, too, because he remained quiet as well. Demetrius kept his attention on his footing and the tracks left by the volunteers. How far ahead were they? Shouldn't they have caught up to them by now?

Another set of trees came between him and Brady. When

Brady came out on the other side, moving in tandem with Demetrius, a large hulking form kept pace on the far side of Brady. The mild anxiety Demetrius had been feeling exploded into full on panic.

"Look out!" Demetrius pointed at the giant, fur-covered being on Brady's opposite side.

"Oh shit!"

Brady literally jumped from his side of the trees to Demetrius's, landing a few inches away. He was in motion even before his feet hit the frozen ground beneath the snow. The creature struggled toward them through the snow, long arms outstretched with hair hanging down. It roared, revealing pointed teeth that looked as if they could tear through flesh.

"What the fuck is that?" Brady's voice went up as he spoke, and he lifted his knees high as he took off through the trees. "What is it?"

"Keep running!" Demetrius followed after Brady, glancing over his shoulder every couple of steps to check on the monster.

Fuck it, he may as well call it what he knew it was: sasquatch. They had gotten separated from the group and were going to be run down and eaten by a fucking sasquatch. Was this what had happened to Cody's father? Was this what Demetrius's life had been leading up to?

"It's gaining on us!" Brady barely missed running into a tree as he looked over his shoulder.

"Just run!"

"Where to?"

"Away from it!"

They had gotten away from the tracks made by the volunteers passing through the woods and were now plunging through snow past their knees. Their progress slowed and Demetrius heard the sasquatch's heavy breathing behind him.

"Faster!" he shouted.

"I'm trying!"

They dodged in and out of trees, their panting breaths streaming behind them. Demetrius didn't dare look over his shoulder. He didn't want to know how much ground it had gained.

A pine tree with a broad sweep of branches came up, and he and Brady went to either side of it. As Demetrius came out, he looked over but did not see Brady. He couldn't have gotten so far ahead he was out of sight. He moved to the side and stopped as he saw Brady on his hands and knees in the snow, struggling to get up.

"Get up!"

"I can't. There's ice under the snow."

The sasquatch came around a tree several yards behind Brady, saw them, and charged.

"Here!" Demetrius waved his arms as he returned to where Brady continued to struggle. Instead of helping him up, Demetrius approached the sasquatch. When it was fifty feet away, he stepped off to the side around a tree. He continued waving his arms as he carefully walked backwards, keeping the beast's attention. It stopped and looked between Brady and Demetrius, trying to decide which of them to go after.

"Stop moving," Demetrius called out.

"Are you fucking crazy? It's like twenty feet away from me!"

"Just hold still, goddammit." Demetrius waved his arms faster. "Come and get me you ugly motherfucker. Yeah, I'm talking to you."

The sasquatch tapped the side of its head where its left ear might be, and Demetrius marveled at how much the movement reminded him of a human. Since it was standing in place, Demetrius lowered one hand to fish his phone out of his coat pocket. The gloves he wore had tiny pads on the fingers to allow him to use his phone without taking them off, and he unlocked it to snap several pictures. When the flash went off, the sasquatch let out a croaky roar, shook its head, and rushed toward him.

"Oh shit." Demetrius turned to run, but the toe of his boot caught on something buried beneath the snow, and he fell to his knees. He put his hands out to cushion his fall, but the snow did that for him. He sank up to his shoulders, his face pressed into the soft, cold snow.

"Fuck!" Demetrius shouted. He expected to feel the sasquatch's big hand come down on his back at any moment and adrenaline flooded his system, allowing him to lunge a good distance off to the side.

"Demetrius!" Brady shouted.

He didn't even look around, just shouted over his shoulder. "Go! Get help!"

The sasquatch was huffing and panting as it approached. Demetrius couldn't get his footing, and his heart banged hard as he gasped and moaned. A red haze of panic dropped over his thoughts. All he could do was try to get to his feet, but he couldn't find any traction.

As the sasquatch approached, one clear thought broke through the fear. Demetrius wished he could have seen Cody one last time and told him again how much he loved him.

CHAPTER TWELVE

"Where's Demmy?"

Cody shaded his eyes as he looked back the way they'd come. The group had come out the other side of the trees and decided to take a break. When he'd gone looking for Demmy, he hadn't been able to find him.

"Who?" a police officer handing out water bottles stopped to look in the same direction as Cody. "Did we lose someone?"

A figure stumbled out of the line of trees. Cody was running back to the trees before he had even thought about it. He could hear people shouting behind him, but all he focused on was the man before him. He could already tell it wasn't Demmy, but as he got closer, he saw it was Brady, and he ran even faster.

"What happened?" He caught Brady as his brother lost his footing and was about to drop face first into the snow. "Where's Demmy?"

"It came after us," Brady said between gulps of air. "He lured it away from me. Told me to run."

"It?" The police officer had caught up to Cody. "What was it?"

"Sasquatch," Brady gasped.

Cody was up and moving again as the officer shouted at him to wait, but Cody wasn't about to wait. He was the more experienced monster hunter in this group of people, probably in the whole damn city.

Fucking monsters. Couldn't they have one trip without something weird or unnatural turning up?

"Demmy!" He entered the woods once more, trying to pick out Brady's tracks from the rest of the volunteers. "Demmy, where are you?"

"Cody?"

His voice seemed to come from all directions, and Cody stopped and cocked his head to listen. "Demmy! Call out again."

"I'm over here."

Cody headed to his left as other members of the search party entered the woods behind him. A few very panicky minutes later, Cody saw Demmy leaning against a tree and let out a relieved laugh. Then he saw the tall figure standing in front of Demmy and his laugh changed to a gasp. He picked up his pace, slowing when he got closer and keeping his gaze on the sasquatch as he stood beside Demmy.

"You okay?"

"Just winded. And a little shaky. This guy scared the hell out of us."

"Sorry," the sasquatch said in a muffled voice, and Cody nearly fell down in surprise.

"It fucking talks?"

"What the living hell is that?" one of the search group shouted.

"It's okay!" Demmy shouted back. "Don't worry. It's just a guy in a costume."

Cody squinted as the sasquatch looked at him. "It's a costume? That's pretty professional."

"Should be," the sasquatch said. "The budget isn't going for our accommodations and meals, that's for sure."

"I'm really lost," Cody said as he finally looked at Demmy. "What's going on?"

"He's a stunt man in a sasquatch movie. He thought we were a couple of actors he was supposed to go after in the scene they're filming today."

"You're kidding me." Cody looked from the sasquatch to Demmy and back again. "Were you out in the woods yesterday too?"

The sasquatch cocked his head. "Nope. They didn't film any sasquatch scenes yesterday. Just interior footage."

"This is really fucking with me," Cody said.

Demmy snorted. "You didn't get chased down by him."

The police officer eased up beside Cody. He had drawn his gun but held it pointed down.

"What's going on?" the officer asked, never taking his gaze off the sasquatch.

"He's a stunt man who got separated from a movie set," Cody said.

"What's your name?" the officer asked, keeping his gun in his hands.

"Augustyn."

The officer holstered his weapon and took a couple of steps toward the sasquatch. He wrinkled his brow as he inspected the face. "Why don't you take the mask off?"

"It's fastened on pretty tight by the make-up crew. We had trouble with the masks coming off during filming, so now I can't take it off myself."

"Where's the crew?" the officer asked.

Augustyn shrugged. "I thought they were in this area, but I guess I got turned around."

"Would they have pulled a permit?" Cody asked.

"Yeah, probably," the officer said as he backed up a couple of steps. "I'll call into the station and find out."

The officer turned away and said to the rest of the volunteers, "Go back to where we stopped and get ready to keep moving. It's just a guy in a suit."

"Is he pulling a prank?" someone asked. "Pretty shitty prank."

"He's part of a movie. Come on now, move along."

"Sorry if I scared you," Augustyn said to Demmy. "I thought it was all part of the scene."

"Well, you're very convincing," Demmy said. "But you weren't in costume yesterday at all?"

"Nope." Augustyn took a step closer. "Did you see a sasquatch yesterday?"

"Not sure," Cody said. "But it's good to rule you out."

"How many different stuntmen have suits like yours?" Demmy asked.

"Three of us."

Cody exchanged a look with Demmy. "Maybe one of them decided to take one out without approval?"

"Couldn't do that very easily," Augustyn said. "They lock up the suits each night in a storage locker where they're keeping most of the props."

"A storage locker?" Demmy chuckled. "Sounds like a real high budget picture."

Augustyn shrugged. "It's paying my rent for a couple of months."

Brady came up on Cody's other side, staring at Augustyn.

"It's a guy in a suit?" Brady said.

"Yep. This is Augustyn."

Augustyn lifted a huge paw. "Hi. Sorry if I scared you."

"Fuck, dude. I nearly shit myself."

"That would have been really gross," Cody said. "Like when you did it back in second grade."

Brady stared at him wide-eyed. "Dude. What the fuck?"

Cody grinned. "What?"

"I nearly had a heart attack a few minutes ago thinking this guy was fucking bigfoot, and you go and bring that up?"

"I don't know, I thought it was pretty funny," Demmy said, and his tone had a little undercurrent of meanness that made Cody wonder what had happened between the two of them.

"How'd you guys fall so far behind anyway?" he asked.

Brady looked away. "We started talking, and then all of a sudden the rest of you were out of sight."

"Yeah, we were talking." Demmy looked toward the sasquatch. "Hey, Augustyn, have you seen a man in his early sixties wandering around looking lost?"

"Other than the director of the movie? Nope, sorry. You lose somebody?"

"My dad's truck went off the road, and we haven't been able to find him," Cody said.

"Aw man, that sucks. Sorry to hear that." A rumbling sound from the area around Augustyn's stomach made him press a fur-covered hand to his belly. "Sorry. I woke up late and skipped breakfast."

"Can you eat inside that costume?" Demmy asked.

"Not really. They have protein shakes for me to drink."

"I gotta tell you, I thought you were the real deal," Demmy said. "You completely got into character."

Augustyn stood up a little straighter, and Cody imagined he could see the guy smile beneath the mask. "Oh yeah? Thanks man, I appreciate that."

"Yeah, you were great," Brady grumbled. He jerked a thumb over his shoulder. "I'm heading back."

"Gotta change your shorts?" Cody asked.

Brady flipped him off as he stomped away.

"I feel really bad about scaring him that much," Augustyn said in a low voice. "Think I should apologize again?"

Cody shook his head. "Not now. Wait until midnight some night and then wear the costume and tap on his bedroom window."

Augustyn snickered. "You his older brother?"

"Does it show?"

"I'm an older brother, too. Totally sounded like something I would suggest." Augustyn shook his head and tapped his ear. "Damn, this earpiece is annoying."

"Earpiece?" Demmy asked.

"The way for the director and assistant to tell me my cues. But this one's been shorting out. That's how I got so lost."

The police officer returned. "Okay, big guy. You need to be about a mile west of here."

"A mile?" Augustyn's shoulders drooped. "Guess I'll get my steps in today at least."

Cody grinned as he looked the suit up and down. "Hey, how tall are you?"

"Six foot eleven," Augustyn said. "Just missed seven feet tall."

"Holy hell," Demmy said. "How do you find pants? And a bed?"

"Online shopping, baby. Well, sorry again for scaring you." Augustyn held out his closed fist and Demmy bumped it. "But it's been nice talking with you. I hope you find your dad. If I hear of any sightings, I'll let the police know." He bumped fists with Cody, then followed the police officer back through the trees.

Cody watched Augustyn's retreating back. "What are the odds?"

"No shit, right?" Demmy shivered. "I'm pretty cold now. Think we could go back to the house?"

Cody nodded. "Absolutely. Let's go."

They started back toward the gas station parking lot in comfortable silence.

"What were you and Brady talking about that got you so behind?"

"Oh, you know, the usual. Questioning my motives for you and me being together, the possibility that I convinced you to be gay over the years. That kind of thing."

Cody stopped in his tracks and looked at him. "Are you fucking kidding me?"

"I wish I were."

"I'm going to kill him." Cody resumed walking, much faster now.

"Before you go on a family murder spree, how about you take a few minutes to calm down?" Demmy was breathing heavily as he tried to keep up. "Come on, slow down. This altitude is killing me."

"Sorry," Cody grumbled, slowing his steps. "What the fuck is wrong with him?"

"The way I understood it, Roman had been talking to him."

"That fucker."

"Yeah, pretty much. But I think I got Brady turned back around."

Cody raised his eyebrows. "You did?"

"I think I did. I kind of went off on him." He made a face. "Sorry about that."

"Are you kidding me? I'm ecstatic." And he was. He wished like hell he'd been there to hear what Demmy said and see Brady's expression, but he was proud of Demmy for standing up for himself.

"Let's get to the car. I'll tell you the details on the way back to the house."

Cody was glad he had borrowed his mother's SUV and driven separately from Grant. His mother, Grant, Roman, and Dave were all still out in the field somewhere, embedded in the line of volunteers. He wondered how Brady had expected to return to the house, then realized he didn't much care. At that moment, he just wanted to get Demmy warm and comfortable.

"Hey, look." Demmy pointed toward the parking lot at least a hundred yards away. "That van at the pumps looks like it might be an equipment van of some kind. Maybe it's from the movie crew."

"You want to audition or something?"

"No. Augustyn hadn't seen your dad, but maybe someone in the crew has seen something. Wouldn't hurt to find out where they're all staying and talk with them. Or suggest the police talk with them, maybe?"

"You're always thinking, aren't you?"

"It's exhausting."

"I'm sure it is. Let's check it out."

Several people stood in line at the register, and Cody couldn't tell which of them might belong to the van. He gestured toward the pumps and said, "Anyone driving that white van?"

A young girl with magenta and lavender hair looked up from her phone with a frown. "I'm driving it. Oh shit, did you hit it?" She walked toward him with a scowl.

"No, nope nope nope. All good out there. Simmer down the rage level. I was just curious if you're working on the movie that's being filmed around these parts?"

She made a disgusted sound. "I wish. I'm a runner for a bakery in town. They send me to fill up the catering vans with gas, get coffee, buy flour. Bullshit like that."

"Well, sorry to bother you. Your van is fine. You can return to Facebook."

"Facebook?" Another sound of disgust as she returned to her place in line. "How old are you? A hundred?"

"Ah, the gentle voices of the younger generation. Thanks for your time."

They exited and headed for the car. Someone left the store behind them and called out, "Excuse me. You were asking about the movie crew?"

A balding man with a dark, full beard heavily streaked with gray approached. He wore a puffy coat with a logo on the breast that read *Killer 'Squatch!* in red letters.

"Hi, yeah," Cody said. "We met up with Augustyn out in the woods. Nice guy."

The man shook his head. "He's kind of a dimwit. And it takes forever to get him to take off that costume. I think he even sleeps in it."

"That's more than a little creepy," Demmy said.

"Tell me about it. We're a small production company, and I'm juggling about five different jobs here. One of them is getting everybody up on time."

"You actually go to every actor's room and wake them up?" Cody asked.

"Yep. And these guys like to drink, so let me tell you, it's not easy some days. Why were you asking about the movie shoot?" He looked Cody up and down. "You're tall, but still a little too short to be a killer 'squatch."

"Darn, there goes my big Hollywood dream."

"Try Phoenix."

"That's where the studio is based?" Demmy asked.

The man nodded. "Just a group of high school friends who met in a Phoenix high school and got some investment capital from their rich parents. The shitty stuff they don't want to do, they hire others to do for them. Like me."

Cody extended a hand. "I'm Cody Bower."

"Tanner Lucas."

"That's an actor's name if I've ever heard it," Cody said.

"Sadly, it's not." Tanner shook Demmy's hand as he introduced himself. "So why were you asking about the crew?"

"My dad's truck went off the road a couple of nights ago

in the snow storm, and we haven't found him yet. I was wondering if you or a member of your crew might have seen someone wandering around. Maybe he hit his head and is lost or something."

"Oh shit, I'm sorry to hear about your dad. I haven't seen anything unusual, nor have I heard any mention from the rest of the crew. I'll ask around though, if you want, and let you know. Do you want to exchange numbers?"

Cody and Tanner added the other's name and number to their contacts. Tanner looked thoughtful as he slid his phone back into his pocket. "You know, one of my jobs is location scout. I know there are a lot of small cabins all around the base of the mountains. Hunting cabins and summer getaways. A number of them can only be accessed by a foot trail."

"Did you go to each one and look it over?" Demmy asked.

"No, that would take too much time. I used a drone and flew it over the areas, then studied the video."

An idea pinged in Cody's brain, and he reached out to shake Tanner's hand once more as he clapped a hand on his shoulder. "Tanner. You've given me a great idea. Thanks for coming out here to talk with us."

Tanner smiled, his teeth bright white inside his graying beard. "I did? That's great. I'll add idea man to my resume."

"You do that. Put me down as a reference," Cody said. "Come on, Demmy. Let's get back to the house."

They hurried to the car, and once inside, Demmy asked, "What's your great idea?"

Cody started the engine and backed out of the space. Once he'd pulled onto the road, he glanced over and asked, "What do you remember about last night?"

Demmy blushed and he looked so damn adorable, Cody wished he could just lean over and kiss him at that very second. But he restrained himself as Demmy cleared his throat and said, "Well, we gave each other blowjobs in the greenhouse office. Then I fell asleep for a bit, and when I woke up I found you in the garage and you fucked me."

"Dammit, I'm getting hard just hearing you talk about it." Cody adjusted himself as he drove. "Do you remember us moving the tarp that covered the patio furniture?"

"Yeah. And it had Christmas gifts hidden under it."

"Right. And one of those gifts is a pretty big drone with a nice high-definition camera on it."

Demmy's face lit up. "We could use that to do a search by air!" He frowned a moment later. "Doesn't the sheriff's department have a drone or something?"

Cody shrugged. "I know they've been using a helicopter, but I would think a drone is a little more maneuverable."

"Yeah, good idea. Whose gifts are those, do you know?"

"From the looks of them, I'd say Roman's."

"What do you mean?"

"They're expensive."

"He's not the only one making money, though. Your parents seem to be doing pretty well out here."

"Good point. Maybe they're gifts my parents got for the kids. Either way, we're going to borrow that drone and make some use of it."

"Have you ever piloted one before?"

"No. But how hard can it be?"

"Oh boy, this is going to be interesting."

"Hey, between the two of us, we can do anything. Right?" Cody smiled as he looked over.

Demmy smiled back. "Right."

CHAPTER THIRTEEN

D emetrius kept quiet and ate his dinner as the Bower family members aired their frustrations with the lack of results from the police and volunteer search.

"Why the hell is it taking so long for them to find him?" Roman said with a ferocious-looking snarl.

"Lots of mountainous spaces to look in, Romes," Grant said. "And so many coniferous trees."

"What are you even talking about?" Roman asked.

"Pine trees," Cody said, staring until Roman looked away.

Demetrius marked a mental point for Cody in the attitude war.

"We've looked in a lot of places with all of those volunteers," Brady said.

"Yeah, speaking of which, where'd you disappear to this afternoon?" Roman asked.

"You left the search, Brades?" Grant said.

Dave looked up from his food. "He told me he didn't feel well. Looks like you're feeling better now from the serving sizes you took."

Brady glanced at Demetrius before looking down at his plate. "Um, yeah. I'm feeling better."

Demetrius felt Cody press his foot press against his beneath the table, and he pressed back. No need to bring anything up at the moment. Brady obviously felt guilty about what he'd said, so Demetrius was willing to let it go. And he didn't see a need to derail the conversation about Mr. Bower with talk of the movie stuntman who had scared them both.

"Tomorrow's Christmas Eve," Dexter said from beside Grant. "Maybe Santa will bring Grandpa home?"

Grant smiled and placed a hand on Dexter's head. "Maybe he will, Dex. You never know what that sneaky guy Santa will do."

"It's statistically impossible for one man to visit every Christian home in one night," Brock stated. "You know that, don't you?"

"Not when there's magic involved," Grant said. "Right Dex?"

"Right!" Dexter's bright smile was like the happy ending to every Christmas movie ever made, and the sight of it lifted Demetrius's spirits a bit.

After dinner, Demetrius helped dry dishes before Cody tipped his head toward the back door. He followed Cody out to the garage, assuming they were going to climb the steps to Grant's apartment. But Cody opened the side door to the garage at the bottom of the stairs and stepped inside.

"What are we doing?" Demetrius looked back toward the house to make sure no one was watching.

"We've got one more day to find my dad," Cody said, waving him inside. "And it's time to take matters into our own hands."

"You're sure about this drone idea?"

"Yep. Let's see what that thing can do."

Over an hour later, Demetrius yawned and rubbed his

eyes. He was tired and couldn't focus on the tiny print of the instruction manual. Cody sat in one of the padded chairs, his elbows on the glass-topped patio table and the mostly assembled drone squatting before him like some kind of over-sized alien bug. It was square, a foot long on all sides with a propeller on each corner.

"Fucking thing won't connect to my phone. Why the fucking hell is this so difficult? This is a kid's toy." Cody put his head in his hands. "It should not be this difficult."

"It's actually a little more complicated than the smaller ones we've seen at the discount stores," Demetrius said.

Cody glared at him, and Demetrius raised both hands in surrender before going back to the instruction manual. He looked for the section about connecting to a smart phone and read through it. "Do you have Bluetooth switched on?"

"Yes, Bluetooth is on." Cody picked up his phone and looked at it. He gave Demetrius a quick glance before tapping the screen. "Yes. Bluetooth is on."

"Do you mean Bluetooth is on now that I reminded you to check it?"

"Okay, the drone camera is connecting to my phone." Cody smiled, but he looked as tired as Demetrius felt. "What's next?"

"How about we go to bed? We've been hiding out here ruining one of your niece or nephew's Christmas presents for a while now."

"We're not ruining Christmas. If this works, we're going to make it twice as awesome because we'll have their grandfather back."

Demetrius set the instruction manual aside. "What do you think happened to him?"

Cody sat back and folded his hands over his stomach. He looked sad and tired, and Demetrius felt bad asking him the question, but maybe it was best for him to talk about it.

"I don't know where he is, but I get the feeling he's still alive."

"It's been a long time," Demetrius said carefully. "And there have been two snow squalls since the accident."

"I know, and that's what makes this drone idea even more important."

One of the garage doors started to go up, startling both of them. Demetrius jumped to his feet, feeling guilty, but he had no idea what to do or where to go, so he just stood rooted in place as Cody's mother pulled her small SUV into the garage. Cody picked up the drone, turned right and left, then gave up and set it back down on the table. He looked at Demetrius and shrugged as they waited to be discovered.

Cody's mother stepped out of the SUV and walked to the back. She opened the tailgate and reached in to grab a couple of reusable grocery bags. When she stepped back from the SUV, she turned toward them and gave a little shout of surprise.

"Hellfire and brimstone, you scared the devil out of me."

"Sorry Mom, didn't mean to."

"What are you boys doing out here in the garage?" She caught sight of the drone and her eyes widened. "Cody Duran Bower, what have you done? That drone was a gift for Brock!"

"I know, and I'm sorry. But I've got an idea to help find Dad."

Her mouth snapped shut and she gave him a hard stare. "Dozens of volunteers have been out walking through deep snow and thick woods looking for your father. The police have flown helicopters over the entire county, but no one has seen a single clue. You just ruined Brock's Christmas with some cockamamie idea you can step in and save the day all by yourself. Well, I hate to be the one to burst your bubble, but it's not going to happen. Your father is either dead and frozen stiff under the snow out there—"

"Jesus, Mom!" Cody said.

"—or he's run off and left us all to find some new life. Who knows? I certainly don't, and I don't think any of you boys know either. Because sometimes a man thinks about things he never intends to tell anyone about, not even his wife of almost forty years."

She let out a deep, hitching sob and rushed out of the garage.

Demetrius stared at Cody who stared back. They blinked and looked at the open garage door then back at each other.

"What the fuck was that about?" Cody asked.

"You know, I'm remembering something just now." Demetrius sat on the chaise lounger and tapped a finger against his chin. "When your mom and I smoked that joint in Hemp House, I remember her talking about your dad being upset with her. But right as she started to tell me about it, you found us." He looked at Cody as he struggled to remember what she had said. The High Altitude had really relaxed him, and made him more than a little horny, so he hadn't been paying as much attention as he should.

"Dude, you can't just say something like that and not follow it up with the actual thing she said."

"Yeah, I know, I'm sorry. Only a hint of it came back to me, and I shouldn't have said anything." Demetrius gestured toward the open garage door. "Think you should go after her?"

Cody shuffled his feet as he looked toward the door. "I guess I should."

"No guesses. You really need to talk with her."

With a heavy sigh, Cody grabbed his coat and started for the open door. He paused to look back at Demetrius. "Want me to close the door?"

"Yes, please."

One more miserable sigh before Cody stepped outside

past the door sensors and reached back in to hit the button. The door lowered, cutting off the view of Cody trudging toward the house.

Demetrius looked at the drone on the patio table. Taking the instruction manual with him, he sat in the chair Cody had vacated and started to read.

IT WAS ALMOST ten when Demetrius hit the door open button. The cascade door rolled up, and he carried the drone into the clear, cold night air. A few of the windows at the house glowed with lamplight, and he wondered how Cody's talk with his mother was going. He'd been gone a little more than an hour now, and Demetrius had stayed in the garage, giving them some space and working on the drone. He'd managed to connect his phone to the camera, and now he was ready for a test flight. He just wished Cody was there as well.

He set the drone on a section of the driveway where the snow had been plowed clear and checked to make sure the propellers spun freely. This drone was piloted by a controller with two small joysticks on either side, and a USB plug in for a mobile phone cable to display and record the camera images. With the controller in hand, Demetrius took several steps back and hit the power button. A moment later, the image from the camera appeared on his phone.

Carefully working the joysticks with his thumbs, Demetrius got the propellers spinning and laughed as the drone slowly lifted into the air.

"Holy shit, you got it flying!"

Cody rushed toward him along the path leading to the back door of the house, zipping his coat and pulling on his hat and gloves.

"I did!" Demetrius's distraction caused the drone to dip

and fly to his right, headed directly for the side of Hemp House. "Oh, shit!"

He worked the levers as he repeated "Oh, shit," like a mantra, but the drone only wobbled faster toward the greenhouse, directly at one of the windows. To save the glass, Demetrius pulled both levers down, sending the drone into the snow.

"What the hell happened?" Cody asked, hurrying toward the crash site.

"I couldn't control it," Demetrius said. "Rather than break a window on the greenhouse and wreck Grant's plants, I dropped it into the snow."

Cody picked up the drone and inspected it as he carried it back to where Demetrius stood.

"It doesn't look busted," Cody said.

"That's good. I did the only thing I could think of."

"Let me give it a shot."

Demetrius handed over the controller and watched as Cody floated the drone high up into the night sky. The camera showed the Bower house with some windows spilling light onto the snow. He flew it over the garage and back again, then took it down the dark road a short distance before bringing it back.

"Man, this is pretty awesome," Cody said. "We need to get one for the office."

"What would we use it for?"

"Are you kidding? We could fly it up into trees and look for critters, or check out the roofs of houses to look for critter entry points."

"That might work for a write off."

"Yes!" Cody's grin made him look like a kid, and Demetrius laughed.

The side door of the house opened, and Alice leaned out with a heavy sweater wrapped tight around her.

"Put that thing away," she said in a loud whisper. "At least keep it out of sight of Brock so he can be surprised on Christmas!"

"Sorry, Mom." Cody brought the drone back and executed a bumpy landing on the driveway before them.

"Sorry, Alice."

"Get it inside before he looks out the window," she said.

"We're going," Cody said. "Sorry."

He handed Demetrius the controller and picked up the drone, leading the way back inside the garage. They looked at each other and managed to hold in their laughter until the door had shut behind them. Demetrius laughed so hard his eyes watered, and he had to take off his coat to keep from overheating.

"It was like we were ten again and got caught doing something bad," Demetrius said.

Cody chuckled as he looked the drone over. "All grown up, but still in trouble."

"You're just a big handful of trouble."

"That sounds pretty dirty."

Demetrius shook his head and grinned. "You can make anything sound dirty."

"Hey, you said it, not me."

"I take it you approve of how the drone works?"

"Yeah. I think we may be able to cover a lot more ground this way."

"I agree. Hey, did your mom tell you anything about her and your dad?"

Cody lifted his shoulders in a quick shrug. "Kind of, but not really. She just said something about how forty years of a marriage builds up a lot of history, and sometimes that can be a bad thing. Then she told me to make sure you would make me happy before we got really serious. She said it wouldn't be fair to you if I decided to become a swinger."

As Cody snorted and shook his head, the word 'swinger' kicked off a memory for Demetrius. When he and Alice had been in the Hemp House office, she had mentioned something about swings just before Cody had arrived. Demetrius thought she had been talking about actual swings for some reason, but now he suspected she had been referring to couples sex. He swallowed past a nervous lump in his throat as he looked at Cody who was inspecting the drone.

Demetrius made a face as he considered his options. Should he say something? He didn't have any real answers for Cody, but it might help him understand what was going on between his parents. He hesitated, nearly avoided saying anything, then finally said, "I just remembered something your mom said to me in the office."

Cody cocked an eyebrow. "Oh? Why do you look so nervous about it?"

He took a step closer and lowered his voice. "Do you think your parents could have an open marriage?"

Cody's expression was blank for a few moments, as if his brain had to process the concept. Then he sneered with disgust and said, "Ew, gross, Demmy. What the hell did you say that for? No one likes to think about their parents having sex with each other, let alone different people."

"Well, yeah, I get that. But during our conversation she mentioned something to me about her and your dad… um, swinging."

Cody's expression of shock and disgust nearly made Demetrius laugh.

"What?" Cody said. "Like in leather swings or something?"

"Jesus, no. Swinging like the term for an open marriage."

"God, I really did not need those images in my head just before trying to get to sleep." He studied the drone in his hand and twirled each propeller with a finger. After a moment he looked up at Demetrius. "Do you really think that's what she said?"

"Pretty sure about it. Sorry."

"Maybe they had a fight about it, huh? And that's why Dad took off in the truck?"

"That could explain it." Demetrius had a thought and started to say it, then closed his mouth.

But Cody had been watching and knew him too well. "What?"

Demetrius tried to look innocent. "What what?"

"You were going to say something then stopped."

"I was?"

"Demmy…"

"Fine. It was just a thought, so it's not based on evidence."

"Noted. What was this non-evidence based thought?"

"What if the reason no one picked us up at the airport and things were really hectic at the house when we arrived is because one of their couples was here?"

Cody's jaw dropped. "You think my parents were getting their freak on just before their kids arrived for Christmas?"

Demetrius lifted one shoulder in a half shrug. "I don't know, maybe. It might have been a way for them to relax before all the craziness of the holiday. It would explain why Grant kept us out of the house when we first arrived and took us right out to the greenhouse."

"Oh my God. I can't…" Cody looked a little ill as he turned in a circle. "The images won't leave. I can't get them out of my head."

"Let's not jump to conclusions though, okay?"

Cody stopped turning in place and stared at him. "If that is what happened, it means Grant knows about it."

"Cody…"

"He knows about it and hasn't said anything."

"At the risk of sending you off into more of a rage, I'm

going to suggest it really isn't his place to say anything, you know? This is between your mom and dad."

Cody scowled. "Yeah. But it still pisses me off."

"Understandable. But, again, we don't know anything for sure."

"For the love of… Merry fucking Christmas, you know?"

Demetrius took the drone from him and set it aside then pulled him into a tight hug. "I know. I'm sorry." He stepped back and caught Cody's gaze. "And it's not the end of the world. So what if your parents have a polygamous relationship? They're still together, and your mom is obviously very worried about your dad. As long as they talk openly with each other how they feel about it, I think it's great."

Cody frowned. "Great?" He shuddered slightly. "Come on, Demmy, it's my parents. Gross."

"I know, but they're making it work."

"I guess." Cody met his gaze a moment before looking away. "Is it something you'd want?"

Nerves tightened Demetrius's stomach. Oh shit, where was this going? Was this kind of arrangement something Cody wanted? "Me? An open relationship? Well, I don't know. I guess it would depend on the situation and the person I was involved with." He swallowed hard and forced the words out. "Is it something you'd want?"

"I can barely keep dates and times straight for just one person," Cody said. "I'm not good trying to balance multiple partners. I'd probably just end up pissing everyone off."

Cool relief swept through Demetrius, and he smiled. "Nice you have that insight."

Cody gave him a long, serious look. Demetrius was about to ask what he was thinking when Cody pulled him into another hug, practically clinging to him. "I've had a lot of insights lately. And I'm sorry Brady said those things to you earlier today. He shouldn't have said that shit."

Demetrius moved back. "Don't worry about it."

"But I do worry about it. My brothers are mostly useless, but they grew up with you around all the time. I'm surprised how Brady reacted."

Demetrius grinned. "But not Roman?"

Cody grunted. "I would have been surprised at any other reaction from him."

"He's always been wound a little tight."

"Yeah. But Brady's pretty easy going."

"People change as they get older. He's living on his own, he has new friends and co-workers, plus he's expecting a baby. That can all change someone's outlook."

"He shouldn't have said those things to you, though."

Demetrius hesitated but finally decided to say what he was thinking. "I know you've said before you've been attracted to other men in the past but never had sex. Why did you decide to take things to the next step with me?"

Cody looked almost angry, and Demetrius immediately regretted his words. He wanted to take a step back as Cody approached, not because he felt threatened, but to give him space. Apparently Cody had other ideas and grabbed Demetrius by the upper arms and pulled him close for a heavy-duty kiss. When he finally pulled back, Cody kept tight hold of him and looked into his eyes.

"Those other guys never knew me as well as you do. And they didn't make me laugh like you do, and they didn't make me mad like you do, and they didn't look as fucking adorable in the morning as you do. I went out on dates, and I kissed a few guys, but I never took it any farther because it didn't feel right. I was the same way with women, believe it or not. If I didn't feel a spark of something beyond a physical attraction with a woman, I didn't let things go too far."

Demetrius's heart pounded, and his chest felt tight. "Oh. So, you're saying there's a spark between us?"

Cody smirked before leaning in to kiss him again, slower and deeper this time. Afterwards, he rested his forehead against Demetrius's and said, "There's a fucking forest fire between us, Demmy. You'd better get used to having me around."

Demetrius laughed quietly and kissed him again. "Sorry for asking. I just needed to make sure I didn't turn you gay."

"You turned me happy, and gay is another term for happy, so in some aspects, yes, you turned me gay. But not the way Roman meant it, and not the way Brady was hinting at." He kissed him again, quick and soft. "Come on, we've both been thinking way too much tonight. Let's go stretch out on Grant's living room floor and get some sleep."

"I think that's a great idea."

Demetrius hid the drone under the tarp and followed Cody out of the garage and up the steps.

CHAPTER FOURTEEN

Cody barely managed to look his mother in the eye the next morning when he asked to borrow her SUV. She was distracted by the grandkids and didn't ask him where he was headed, just handed him the keys from her purse. After stowing the drone and controller in the back of the SUV, Demmy got in the passenger seat, and Cody got behind the wheel. He backed out of the garage and down the long drive toward the road. Grant was walking toward them from the greenhouse and waved. Cody lifted his hand in return but didn't stop the car to talk. He wasn't ready to talk to Grant yet. Even though he knew none of this was Grant's fault, Cody couldn't help feeling hurt that Grant and his parents hadn't trusted him enough to tell him what was going on.

Though, to be fair, he hadn't trusted any of them with his own personal relationship issues, so he really couldn't throw stones.

"Make a left at this next road," Demmy said as he looked at his phone, then stifled a yawn. "Sorry."

"We're going to need a pot of coffee each to stay awake."

"Just keep telling yourself it's two hours later back home, and we'd be up already."

Cody snickered. "Good luck getting that to work for you."

"Yeah. I know." Demmy moved the GPS map around. "How'd you come up with this location to launch the drone?"

"Just kind of half-ass guessed it based on where my dad's truck went off the road and where the police and volunteers have searched already."

"And your mom's okay with what we're doing?"

"She didn't ask any questions, so I'm not sure she even suspects what we're doing. I didn't tell any of my brothers because I didn't want to get into it with them."

"Where do they think we've gone this morning?"

"I didn't say, so whatever they want to suspect is what it will be."

"Leaving them guessing on Christmas Eve, eh?"

"Something like that. It's part of the magic of the season."

"What time is dinner planned for tonight?"

Cody glanced at him. "You hungry already?"

"Not yet. But I am looking forward to a big meal."

"No one said anything, but I'm assuming something like five o'clock."

"Gives us plenty of time to do some scouting by drone. Oh, turn right up here."

They bounced along the narrow road. It was not maintained by the county, so it had not been plowed. Other vehicles had passed through since the last snowfall, and Cody followed the tracks left behind. He gripped the steering wheel tight as the trail climbed higher, and the ground to their right fell away.

"That's a long way down," Demmy said as he scooted as far from the passenger door as he could and stared wide-eyed out the window.

"We'll be a little bit higher before we get to the turn-offs I saw on the map."

"I hope they're on your side of the road. This view is making me a little woozy."

"I marked the spot on the GPS. How much farther?"

Demmy checked the phone. "Less than a mile."

A few minutes later, Cody nearly drove past what looked like a driveway. Trees grew to either side of it, and someone had plowed or shoveled away snow down to gravel. He turned into the trail and slowly drove up a short hill, made a sharp left turn at the top, and pulled into a small gravel lot that had also been cleared.

"Someone's been out here taking care of this area," Demmy said.

"Lucky for us." Cody turned the engine off. "Ready?"

"Let's do this."

They left the SUV, and Cody opened the tailgate so they could work on the drone. In a few minutes, they had Cody's phone setup in the controller and the drone connected and powered up. Demmy carried it out to the road, and Cody fiddled with the joysticks. When Demmy returned to his side near the back of the SUV, Cody smiled and said, "Here we go."

"Good luck."

"Yeah. No kidding."

Cody started the propellers and edged the drone into the air. It wobbled and canted right to left as he fought against the wind and got comfortable with the controls once again. The camera was pointed in their direction, and he saw Demmy and himself standing side-by-side in the video feed on his phone.

"Easy there," Demmy said.

"Harder than it looks in videos."

"It always is."

After a few more adjustments, Cody directed the drone across the road out into the open space beyond the drop off. The video image gave him a bit of vertigo as the snow-covered ground fell away, but he managed to focus more on steering the drone. Before long, he felt pretty accomplished as he flew it over wooded areas and wide, snowy plains.

"Look at you, drone pilot," Demmy said.

"Yeah, I think I'm getting the hang of it."

Cody directed the drone in wider and wider circles. Trees and massive chunks of granite went past on the screen of his phone. On the far side of a stand of trees, Cody caught a glimpse at the same time as Demmy of something that might have been a small shelter.

"There," Demmy said, pointing at the phone. "What was that?"

"I saw it," Cody said as he shifted away from Demmy. "You're blocking the screen."

"Sorry."

"Don't be a backseat drone driver."

"Cute."

Cody smirked and waggled his eyebrows as he kept his gaze on the screen and maneuvered the drone back around. "You've been saying I'm cute a lot lately."

"Because you've been acting cute."

"Don't start flirting with me right now," Cody said. "We don't have time to follow through."

"Not even for a quickie?"

He shot a glance at Demmy to see if he was serious and found him grinning. "Tease."

"Let's find your dad, then we'll celebrate."

"Where will we celebrate?"

"We could always use the garage again."

"That was pretty fun." Cody turned the drone and was

about to take it past the trees again when it suddenly veered off course.

"What did you do?" Demmy asked.

"That wasn't me!"

Demmy crossed the road and stood a few feet back from the edge of the drop-off, shielding his eyes as he stared out across the snow gleaming in the sunlight. He gasped and pointed. "There! It looks like an eagle attacked the drone."

"Are you fucking with me?"

"Not even a little bit."

"Shit, I can't get it to straighten out. That fucking bird must have taken out a propeller."

"The eagle's coming around again." Demmy returned to his side. "Can you fly the drone between a couple of trees and lose it?"

"How about I set it down in the snow?"

"Won't the eagle land on it?"

"This is why we can't have nice things."

"Well, this and money," Demmy said. "But that's beside the point."

"Okay, I'm going to stay low and head for the—"

The image on Cody's phone spun and tilted heavily to the side.

"Ah!" Cody shouted. "I'm hit!"

Moments later, it was all over. Cody's phone showed all white as the drone plummeted into the deep snow just outside the stand of trees.

"Where'd it go down?" Cody asked.

Demmy stepped out onto the road, one hand over his eyes as he stared out across the snow. A horn sounded, startling both of them. Cody shouted, "Look out!" as Demmy jumped forward to the opposite side of the road and out of the path of the jacked up pick-up truck with fat tires. The truck rumbled past, leaving a rooster tail of snow and gravel behind. Cody turned away from the snow that blew into his face, and when the truck had gone around the bend, looked to where Demmy stood.

Or rather, where Demmy should have been standing.

"Demmy?"

Cody ran across the road without pausing to look for traffic. He saw several sets of footprints leading to and from the edge of the drop-off, and then the ragged edges of broken hard-packed snow. His gut knotted in fear as the skin of his scalp prickled.

"Demmy!"

He tossed the controller aside and dropped to his hands and knees, crawling forward to peer over the edge. The decline was steeply sloped, and he followed the impression Demmy's body had made as he slid down it. At the bottom of the slope, Cody could see Demmy laying spread-eagle on his back. He estimated it was about a height of three stories, and he had just opened his mouth to call out to him when the snow under his hands gave way.

His shout of surprise was cut off by a rush of snow battering his face and pushing into his mouth. He closed his eyes and clamped his mouth shut as he slid down the slope on his belly, bouncing over bumps in the snow and hoping he didn't break his neck. The force of his slide took him a few feet past where Demmy lay before he eventually slowed to a stop. Snow was jammed inside his coat, shirt, and, oddly, his pants. He was cold all over as he spit out snow and struggled to stand.

"What the fuck just happened?"

Demmy's groggy voice brought Cody around, and he staggered back a few steps to drop into a seated position beside him.

"We just became human toboggans."

Demmy sat up slowly and stretched his neck left then right. "Ow."

"You hurt?"

"I've got snow packed in all sorts of weird places. But I don't think I'm hurt." He looked up the hill. "How the hell are we going to get back up there?"

"We'll have to walk back to the road and hike up the trail." He looked out over the wide expanse of field. "But we'll need to go and fetch the drone first."

"Can't you just fly it back to us?"

"I think the eagle damaged it too badly. Plus, I dropped the controller at the top of the hill."

"Oh." Demmy looked up the hill again. "It's pretty much impossible for us to climb back up there, isn't it?"

"Unless you've been bitten by a radioactive mountain goat recently, I'm going to say yeah, it's pretty much impossible."

Demmy searched his pockets then swore. "I don't have my phone."

"Did you lose it when you slid down the hill?"

"I don't know. I may have left it in the car. I think I set it aside before we got out, but I don't remember for sure."

"I hope so. And I hope no one comes by and steals the controller and my phone while we're down here trekking around like Admiral Byrd."

Demmy looked impressed. "Did you just make a reference to someone we learned about in social studies?"

"Hey, I paid attention sometimes."

Demmy's expression shifted to doubtful. "Yeah?"

Cody got to his feet and extended a hand to pull Demmy up. They opened their coats and shook out what loose snow had not yet melted, then zipped up again.

"How far do you think it is?" Demmy asked.

"Can't be more than a mile, right?"

"Okay, let's get moving."

"Hey." Cody grabbed Demmy's hand and held him back.

Demmy looked up at him. "Yeah?"

Cody gave him a soft kiss. "Here's to another adventure."

That earned him a grin. "Yeah. We've had quite a few of them. Life with you is never dull."

"You're welcome."

Cody kissed him once more before they set off. The snow was past their knees, and it hampered their progress. They complained about it at first, but after a short time, they were breathing too heavily to talk much. When they finally reached the spot where the drone had gone down, both were panting and sweaty.

"That was a hell of a cardio workout," Cody said.

"It's the latest fitness craze. Just fill an empty building with three feet of snow and have people walk back and forth."

"Toss in some penguins, and you've got a hit."

"I'll make a note." Demmy looked up into the sky. "No sign of the eagle. And it looks like it's late morning now."

Cody picked up the drone and looked it over. "One of the propellers is totally mangled. I'm going to owe Brock a new drone. I wonder how much these things cost?"

"A hell of a lot more than we have, I'm sure." Demmy looked into the woods a few yards away. "Hey, that thing we saw on the camera is back there. Is it a cabin?"

Cody looked and saw a shelter of sorts, but he wasn't sure he would call it a cabin. It was just plywood hammered together with a piece of corrugated sheet metal laid over top on an angle to allow for run-off of melted snow. A rusted stovepipe stuck up from a back corner of the roof with smoke streaming out of it. It didn't have any windows, but a camou-flage-painted door had been installed in the wall facing them.

"It looks like the place where the monsters live that haunt every kid's nightmares," Cody said.

"There's smoke coming from the stovepipe," Demmy said.

"And?"

"And maybe we should check it out, since we're right here."

"How many horror movies start this way?"

"All of them." Demmy started toward the woods.

"Fuck," Cody whispered before following.

Just as they entered the trees, movement off to their left caught Cody's eye, and he froze in place, calling Demmy's name in a loud whisper.

Demmy turned back. "What?"

"Over there." Cody nodded toward the figure moving through the shadows. "What is that?"

Demmy looked and took a step closer to Cody. "It's tall."

"Do you think it could be Augustyn?"

"Augustyn!" Demmy's shout startled a gasp out of Cody, and he nearly dropped the drone.

"What are you doing?" Cody asked in a frantic whisper. The figure in the woods was about fifty feet away. It stopped and turned its big, furry head to look right at him. "Oh, shit."

"Dudes?"

The word floated to them through the trees, and Demmy smiled and shrugged. "See? It's Augustyn, back in costume for *Killer 'Squatch!*"

A rustle of branches from their right made them both turn that way. Cody heard his own high-pitched squeak of surprise echoed by Demmy as a tall, fur-covered figure stepped out from some low-hanging pine branches about fifty yards away.

"Cody and Demetrius, right?" Cody turned to look left as Augustyn approached. "Good to see you guys. I think I'm lost again."

The angry growl from their right made them all turn and look. Even from the greater distance, Cody could tell the new arrival was taller than Augustyn. And from the way it swatted branches out of its way, angrier, too.

"Hey, who's that?" Augustyn asked. "Did that fucking director hire someone new?"

"I don't think that's someone new," Cody said. "I think that's some*thing* new."

"We need to get inside," Demmy added.

"I want to talk to this guy." Augustyn started to walk between them, but Cody grabbed his arm and held him back.

"Dude," Cody said, "that's a real live sasquatch. We need to go."

"No fucking way," Augustyn said in a low voice. "That's bigfoot? This is awesome."

"It's coming closer," Demmy said. "And I don't think we can outrun it."

"Into the cabin," Cody said. "Maybe there's a weapon or something in there."

He pulled Augustyn along as he ran after Demmy toward the cabin. The sasquatch roared as it closed in on them. Cody knew the plywood structure wouldn't stand up against the thing, but they had no other options.

"That thing sounds pissed," Augustyn said, panting as he jogged behind Cody.

"You think?" Cody said.

Demmy had reached the cabin and opened the door. He looked back once to check on their progress before rushing inside. Cody followed without hesitation, hauling Augustyn in behind him. He saw a table with an oil lamp throwing out weak light, a couple of wooden chairs, a cast-iron stove generating heat, and a plywood floor covered with dirty rugs before he turned to slam the door shut. He fumbled with the twist-lock in the knob, securing the door as best he could, and then he turned quickly, intending to grab a chair to brace the door.

Cody nearly screamed when he noticed the figure standing with its back against the rear wall of the one room shack. Then he stopped and stared as his eyes grew accustomed to the dim interior.

"Dad?"

His father smiled and looked embarrassed as he stuffed his hands in the pockets of his coat. "Hi, son."

CHAPTER FIFTEEN

Demetrius looked between Cody and his father. Had they really just stumbled upon Greg Bower out here in a creepy, deserted shack? Had he been there the whole time he'd been missing?

The sasquatch roared from just outside the door, making them all jump.

"It's back!" Cody's father said, eyes wide. "Did it follow you?"

"That lock's not going to hold," Demetrius said.

"Chair." Cody stared at his father a moment longer before looking at Demetrius. "Brace it with a chair."

Demetrius grabbed one of the chairs and wedged it beneath the knob. Seconds later the knob rattled, and he took two big steps back.

"It keeps coming back," Mr. Bower said. "I've been hiding here for days."

"It's a real bigfoot?" Augustyn said.

Mr. Bower looked him up and down. "Who are you?"

"Augustyn." He held out a furry hand.

"Hi," Mr. Bower said, shaking Augustyn's hand and

staring up at him. "Nothing personal, but you're more than a little unsettling."

"And who are you?" Augustyn asked.

"Oh. I'm Greg Bower." He smiled and looked at Cody. "I'm Cody's father."

"Nice to meet you, Mr. Bower."

"Call me Greg."

"Greg it is."

Greg looked him up and down again. "Is this what you wear to go outdoors? Is this your coat? There are a lot of hunters in this area, and that could be very dangerous."

"Oh, no." Augustyn made his fingers into claws and snarled. "I'm a stuntman for the movie *Killer 'Squatch!*"

The sasquatch outside pounded on the door, rattling it in the frame. Demetrius stood by Cody, who was still staring at his father.

"Cody?" he said.

Demetrius's voice seemed to awaken him from some deep introspection, and when he spoke, Cody's words were layered with cool anger.

"You've been hiding out in here this whole time?"

Greg shuffled his feet. "Well, it's a bit more complicated than that, Cody. I'm sure you and your brothers have been worried—"

"Worried?" Cody's laugh was harsh. "People have been looking for you. The police have been looking for you. They've formed search teams and flown helicopters all around here looking for you. And you've been hiding out here in this shitty little shack?"

"Look, son, I'm very, very sorry, but you don't understand all of it."

"All of what, Dad? Huh? What? What exactly are you apologizing for?"

The sasquatch outside growled and snorted as it circled

the shack, pausing now and then to try and pull up an edge of the sheetmetal roof or scratch at a wall.

"Um, guys?" Demetrius said. "Maybe let's keep our voices down so as not to agitate the actual sasquatch that's trapped us in here?"

"Yeah, don't get him too worked up," Augustyn said. "I'd like to study his movements, you know? Kind of get a feel for him to make my performance more genuine."

Greg crossed the small space, arms open as if for a hug, but Cody stepped aside.

"We were all really, really worried. All of us." The hurt in Cody's tone made Demetrius ache for him. He wished he could turn this all around and make finding Greg alive and well a happy situation rather than stressful and angry.

And without an angry sasquatch just outside the door.

"I never meant to do that," Greg said. "It all happened so fast, you know?"

The sasquatch rattled the doorknob again, but the lock held. For now.

"How does it know how to use a doorknob?" Augustyn asked. "Like, how did it learn that?"

"What?" Cody glared at Augustyn. "Jesus God, would you take off that fucking mask? It's ninety degrees in here and just looking at you makes me sweat."

Augustyn shrugged his furry shoulders. "It's kind of affixed to the rest of the suit, and takes a lot of work to get it off."

"Fine, sweat your balls off."

Demetrius lifted the edge of the table to test its weight, then said, "Augustyn, grab the other side of this table, will you? I want to put it up against the door."

"Good thinking."

They carried the table across the room, leaving Cody and his father standing a few feet apart. As Demetrius worked on getting the table up against the door without dislodging the chair under the knob, he listened as Greg explained things.

"I was out for a drive in the truck. That much you know, I'm sure."

"I know a lot more than that, but we can start there. You left the house in a huff and went for a drive, and you went off the road."

Greg looked surprised. "Have you been talking to your mother?"

Cody stepped closer to his father and lowered his voice. "Yeah, Dad, I've been talking to Mom. Mostly trying to console her and tell her everything would work out when you went missing for two nights in the middle of winter right before Christmas. And I know about the… the relationship understanding you two have."

"She told you about it?"

"Not directly, but I know about it. And with all the questions they've been asking, I'd be surprised if the police don't know about it now as well."

Greg gave a derisive snort. "That would be a surprise. Mickey Hastings was just trying to cover everything up."

Demetrius couldn't suppress his gasp as everything suddenly became crystal clear. Helium-voiced Sergeant Mickey Hastings was the other party in Cody's parents' open marriage. He barely managed to keep from shuddering. He glanced at Cody in time to catch his wide-eyed gaze and screwed up his face in what he hoped was an expression of sympathy.

"Sergeant Hastings?" Cody looked at his father. "All of this is because of that squeaky-voiced doofus?"

"Well, not all of it. I initially left the house because of him, but as I was driving along the road, that thing out there—" he waved toward the door "—stepped out in front of me. I clipped it with the side mirror."

Cody met Demetrius's gaze, and they nodded before he looked back at his father. "Demmy found a footprint at the scene and fur on the truck."

Greg looked at him and smiled. "Demetrius. I haven't even said hello to you. It's good to see you."

Demetrius flashed a quick smile and nodded. "Good to see you safe and sound, Mr. Bower."

"Call me Greg."

"Okay. Sure."

Greg smiled and gave a single nod of satisfaction. "So you thought it was a sasquatch from the start? You didn't think it was anything else?"

"We're kind of used to the things that hide in the woods," Demetrius said.

"Really?" Augustyn cocked his head.

The sasquatch outside prowled around the shack once more, testing the walls and roof. Demetrius shivered at the thing's determination and intelligence.

"So you hit the sasquatch," Cody said. "Is that why it's been lurking in the woods in this area?"

"Very possible," Greg said. "After I struck it, I went off the road and hit a tree. I don't remember much right after the crash. I was stunned. When I got my senses back, I saw the sasquatch climbing down to the truck. It was growling and snarling and completely pissed off. My side window had broken in the crash and I was exposed, so I got out of the truck and ran. I was so disoriented, I left my phone behind. I don't know how far it chased me, but I eventually lost it in the snow storm. I was cold and lost, but I eventually found this place.

"Firewood was stacked by the stove, and I found some matches and dehydrated meals, so I holed up here. I heard it come around every now and then, so I never knew when I could make a break for it. I melted snow in a pot on the stove for water, and I sat and thought about things." Greg's eyes shone with tears. "I had only planned to wait until morning and strike out for the nearest road, but it was quiet here and I had everything I needed. It's been years since I've had time to just sit and think like that." He looked at the floor as he practically whispered, "Years."

Cody shook his head, but his tone was more gentle when he spoke. "We've all been really worried about you. We've looked everywhere for you. Mom thinks you're dead."

Greg nodded. "I know I worried you all, and I'm sorry for that. But things have been complicated lately between your mother and me."

"Complicated?" Cody shook his head. "I'd say it's more than complicated. Are you two going to get a divorce?"

"What? No! At least I don't want one. Did you mother say she wants a divorce?"

"No, she's worried sick about you. But this whole…" Cody waved a hand toward his father. "Open marriage thing. It's confusing and sounds like the two of you aren't happy together. As a couple."

"We're happy together," Greg said, looking away with a puzzled expression. "I always thought we were happy. I thought the open marriage would bring us closer, if we shared the experience, you know?"

Despite the situation, Demetrius couldn't help feeling a little anxious about his relationship with Cody as Greg talked. Would this give Cody ideas about their relationship? Would Demetrius be able to handle it if that was what he wanted?

Greg continued. "We agreed to be in it together and stop if either of us didn't like it. We met Mickey and his wife at a couples club in Denver, and it was fun for a while. But then we started just being, well, intimate when we were with them and not on our own, and I found I really missed having that time alone with your mother, you know? I tried to initiate things several times, but something was always more important, or one of the grandkids was around, or we were just both too tired. We only seemed to have the interest and the energy for sex when we got together with Mickey and Connie."

Before Cody could respond, the sasquatch lifted a back corner of the roof with a shriek of screws pulling out of wood. It glared at them through the small space and growled.

"It's going to bust in here," Cody said, turning for the door. "Now's our chance to run."

Demetrius struggled to move the table and the chair. Cody pitched in to help, and Augustyn hauled Greg out of the way as they shoved the heavy table away from the door. The high-pitched sound of more screws pulling free as the beast lifted the roof higher sent shivers down Demetrius's back. Cody tugged the chair from beneath the knob, and Demetrius released the lock and yanked the door open.

The sasquatch stood right outside the door. It let out a deep bellow and ducked beneath the doorframe to grab for them. Demetrius stumbled back out of its reach and bumped into Greg then sat down hard. He heard Greg curse as he lost his balance followed by a yelp of pain from Augustyn. The sasquatch swatted Cody aside, and Cody hit the wall hard, smacking his head against the wood before he groaned and slid down to a slumped sitting position, his legs splayed out before him.

On the floor with his hands braced behind him, Demetrius stared up at the sasquatch as it started to pull itself through the door.

"You stomped on my ankle, man," Augustyn said. "It hurts like a mother—" Augustyn stopped speaking, and Demetrius figured he had just seen the sasquatch filling the entire doorway. "—fucker."

Demetrius scrambled backwards in a crab-walk, gaze

fixed on the massive, furry monster determined to get inside. The smell of it was so rank, his eyes watered and stomach clenched. When the sasquatch finally wedged itself inside, it was too tall to stand upright so it crouched there, blocking their escape and supporting itself with one huge, fisted hand as it looked around the shack. Fur covered it everywhere except for its face, palms, and bottom of its fingers. The hair was matted in a number of places with mud, sticks, and burrs. The leathery skin of its face was criss-crossed with scars, and a bony brow jutted above its deep-sunk eyes. A squashed up nose over dark, thin lips gave it an ape-like appearance.

It looked from Cody, who sat unconscious against the wall, to Demetrius, then its dark yellow eyes shifted to look past him. The anger on the monster's face amazed and frightened Demetrius, and he looked over his shoulder to see Greg standing behind him staring wide-eyed at the sasquatch. At that moment, Augustyn stood up from where he had fallen onto the floor, and Demetrius turned back around, watching the monster's expression shift to something like curiosity. It shuffled a little closer and Demetrius scuttled back from it, his hand coming down hard on something.

"My foot!" Augustyn pulled his foot out from under Demetrius's hand and staggered back.

The sasquatch's eyes widened, and then it glared at Demetrius and howled with anger as it charged him. Demetrius rolled to one side, but the beast grabbed his wrist, bringing him to a jerking stop. Its grip was tight and Demetrius cried out as his bones ground together.

"Hey! Hey!" Greg shouted and waved his arms to get the thing's attention. "It's me you've been looking for the last few days. Remember me? I hit you with my truck. Come get me!"

The room suddenly became much brighter, and Demetrius feared he was close to passing out from the pain in his wrist.

He blinked rapidly in an effort to clear his vision and looked at Cody sitting with his chin on his chest. "Cody!"

Several things happened all at once. Augustyn shrieked, his voice high-pitched and spiked with terror. The light in the room grew even brighter as the smell of burning hair made Demetrius wrinkle his nose, and the sasquatch cried out in alarm and released him as it backed toward the door. Favoring his arm, Demetrius pulled himself to the wall near Cody.

Augustyn screamed as he jumped around the room and waved his arm, which was engulfed in flames. The tipped-over lamp released a wash of burning oil across the tabletop. As Augustyn leaped around, he bumped against the stove and it toppled over, spilling chunks of flaming wood on the floor.

"Fire!" Greg shouted. "Everybody out!"

The sasquatch had tried to escape the shack and was now jammed in the doorway. It stared in terror over its shoulder at the flames on the top of the table, now crawling up the rear wall and across the wood floor.

"Greg, get Augustyn!" Demetrius shouted. "Stop, drop, and roll!"

Greg tried to get Augustyn to hold still, but he was too panicked to listen, so Greg ended up simply tripping the big man as he ran past. Once Augustyn had hit the floor, Greg fell over his burning arm and smothered the flames.

Smoke hung near the ceiling, smelling of Augustyn's scorched costume, the stench of the sasquatch itself, and burning lamp oil and plywood. Demetrius coughed as he shook Cody's shoulder and patted his cheeks.

"Cody, wake up. Oh, you gotta wake up. Come on."

Cody groaned and lifted his head, peering around blearily until he found Demetrius. "Demmy?"

"We gotta go. Stand up."

"What's going on?" Cody's eyes widened. "Fire!"

"Yep. Let's go."

"Where's my dad? Dad!"

"He's okay, he's right over there. Get up."

Cody pushed to his feet and swayed unsteadily. "Whoa."

Demmy put an arm around his waist to hold him up, grunting at the exertion. "Easy, big guy."

Greg and Augustyn got to their feet, and all four looked at the sasquatch, struggling to figure out how to escape through the door.

"We're not getting out that way," Cody said.

Flames climbed the back wall and a knot in the wood popped, making all of them jump.

"The wall." Augustyn pointed right at Demetrius and Cody. "We could push it down maybe?"

"Let's try it," Demetrius said.

He put his hands against the side wall as Cody did the same. Sweat poured down his face and coated his back. Heat pushed down on them from the metal roof as flames crackled and popped a dozen feet away. The stovepipe had pulled out of the ceiling when the stove had fallen over, allowing a good portion of the smoke to escape, but Demetrius could feel it thickening quickly.

"Push!" Cody shouted, and all four of them shouted with the effort.

But the wall didn't even budge, and they dropped to their knees, gasping for breath.

"We're trapped!" Greg said.

The sasquatch made a high-pitched keening noise. Its mouth was open, and its eyes so wide Demetrius could see white all around the dark yellow irises. It turned its back to them and banged its fists against the front wall. The wood frame shuddered, and the foot of the wall bumped out several inches.

"It's going to push through the front wall," Demetrius said. "Get ready to run!"

"Move up, the fire's closer," Augustyn said.

They crawled forward as the monster battered the front wall. Cody was a few feet behind the sasquatch when he stopped, causing all of them to pile up behind him.

"He's almost through," Cody said over his shoulder.

The wall cracked beneath its pounding fists, and then it split down the middle. The monster snarled as it punched the wall apart and finally shoved its way outside.

"Now!" Cody shouted.

He ran in a stooped-over position, Demetrius following. He was close to passing out from the heat and smoke and hoped he had enough energy to make it outside. But a wave of dizziness crashed over him, and he stumbled the last few feet. The splintered ends of the plywood wall snagged his coat sleeve as he slipped outside, and it brought him up short. Greg and Augustyn crawled past him, coughing and gagging as they collapsed in the snow.

"I'm stuck," Demetrius said between coughs. He tried to get himself loose, but he was weak from the heat and smoke and couldn't quite get it.

"Dad, you okay?" Cody asked.

"Help me," Demetrius said, but his voice was dry and husky and didn't carry far. "Cody. Hey, Cody."

More coughing, and still he couldn't get free. He felt the fire approaching when a shape rose up beside him, and he let out a breath of relief. Cody had come to help him at last.

"Hey, I'm stuck."

Demetrius looked up, then looked higher. At first he thought it might be Augustyn, because all he saw was dark fur. But when the smell hit him, he knew it was the sasquatch.

"Cody!" The name exploded out of him, and he heard

Cody shout, but everything else got lost as Demetrius struggled to pull his coat free from the jagged wood.

The sasquatch roared, the flames behind Demetrius perfectly illuminating the thing's terrifyingly angry expression. Panic infused Demetrius's muscles with adrenaline, and he yanked free of the wood just as the sasquatch grabbed for him. He moved to the side, feeling its fingers skim over his jacket.

"Get back!"

Cody was beside him, waving a burning piece of wood at the beast and shouting for it to get away. The thing snarled and jumped back, hunkering down in the snow and glaring at them.

"You okay?" Cody asked.

"Yeah. My jacket got caught, but I'm okay."

"Ready to move? We gotta get away from the fire."

"Let's go."

Cody put an arm around him, and Demetrius didn't think anything had ever felt so good. With the burning wood held out toward the sasquatch, Cody helped Demetrius back to where Greg and Augustyn waited.

"Now what?" Augustyn asked. "If we try to make a run for it, that thing will chase us down."

Cody looked at him, and then did a double take. "Dude. You can do it."

Demetrius looked at Augustyn and understood immediately what Cody had in mind. The fur around Augustyn's face had been singed, and some of the latex features of his face had melted from the heat of the fire, making him look even more frightening.

"Yeah," Demetrius said. "You can scare the thing off."

"What? Dudes, I'm, like, not a real sasquatch. You know that, right?"

"It does appear to be curious about you," Greg said. "Maybe you could get closer and startle him."

"Get *closer*?" Augustyn's voice went up an octave at the end.

The back wall of the shack collapsed in a fireworks display of sparks, leaving the remaining walls leaning precariously inward beneath the metal roof.

"At least the fire won't have a chance to spread with all this snow," Greg said.

"Yeah, and once it burns out, we'll freeze if we can't make it back to the car," Cody said.

"Oh, which car did you bring?" Greg asked.

"What?" Cody frowned. "Mom's car."

Greg smiled and said, "I do like that car," as Demetrius restrained himself from shouting at Greg to shut up about the car.

Cody wasn't going to play nice, however. "We have something much more important to deal with than what car we drove to get here."

The monster stood up and growled, lifting its arms overhead. They all cowered back from it, Demetrius pressing himself against a tree. He was terrified the thing would charge them at any moment and start pounding the shit out of them all.

"Rawr!"

Demetrius saw Augustyn on his feet, his arms extended high and fingers curled into claws. The rubber padding on his face had sprung up in some spots, and the fur on his head stood in corkscrews. The fur along his arms had come loose and flapped in the wind. He really did look frightening.

Demetrius jumped as a loud, guttural roar echoed through the woods. The sasquatch dropped into a squat and grabbed handfuls of snow, broken branches, leaves, and pieces of wood it threw into the air. It stood and pounded on its chest then hammered on the trunk of a tree. The blows it struck on the tree were so strong snow fell onto it from the branches above. Wind caught some of the falling snow and dusted all of them in a cold and sparkly coating.

"Oh shit," Augustyn whispered. "I made it really mad."

The sasquatch suddenly rushed at them. Everyone shouted and jumped out of the way. In the confusion, the sasquatch lost its footing in the snow and slid head-first into the tree behind them, bringing down a cascade of snow. Snow slid down the back of Demetrius's neck and along his spine, and he gasped as he scrambled to get to his feet. Augustyn was crawling toward the burning shack in an effort to get away while on the other side of the sasquatch, Cody helped his father get to his feet.

With a groan and a shake of its shaggy, snow-dusted head, the sasquatch rolled over onto its back. Its breath sent a plume of snow and vapor into the cold air. With another groan, it sat up and looked right at Demetrius, its hands lying loosely in its lap.

A chill went through Demetrius. He took a slow step backwards, and then another.

"Cody," he said in a loud whisper, not taking his eyes off the sasquatch sitting before him.

"What… Shit." From the corner of his eye, Demetrius saw Cody fidget in place.

"I don't know what to do," Demetrius said.

"Just keep backing slowly away from it," Cody said. "Dad and I will move back too."

The sasquatch watched his cautious retreat from under heavily lidded eyes. Demetrius figured it had hit its head pretty hard on the tree and might have a concussion. He wondered how that might affect the beast's behavior, but he realized he didn't much care. All he wanted was to be as far away from the thing as possible.

As he put more distance between them, Demetrius felt the tiniest spark of hope he might be able to get away. He figured he could meet up with Augustyn, and they could circle around the shack and join Cody and Greg then all of them could escape. Things might turn out all right after all. Cody's dad had been found, and despite the loss of the drone inside the mysterious plywood shack, Demetrius thought they would get back to the house in one piece.

The backs of Demetrius's knees hit something and he fell over it, pinwheeling his arms to try and stay upright. He landed on his back in the snow and looked to see what he had tripped over, finding Augustyn lying flat on his stomach, looking at him.

"Dude, you fell on me."

"You tripped me."

The sasquatch snorted, getting to its feet and advancing on them. Its hands were tight fists the size of Demetrius's head, and he did not want to know how it felt to get hit by one of them.

"Up!" Demetrius shouted. "Run!"

He scrambled to his feet, helped Augustyn stand, and they ran along the side of the shack. The sasquatch stomped after them, fists swinging. The heat from the fire had melted the snow behind the shack, and they waded through puddles of muddy water.

When the sasquatch rounded the back corner of the shack and roared at them from a few feet away, both Demetrius and Augustyn jumped. Augustyn turned and raised his arms overhead again as he said, "Rawr!" His voice was quiet and trembling, and it seemed to only piss the sasquatch off even more. It let out an even louder, angrier bellow before taking a swing at Augustyn. Moving faster than Demetrius would have expected, Augustyn stepped back out of the path of the sasquatch's fist, and it struck the back corner post of the shack. The burning post snapped, and the corrugated metal sheeting roof collapsed to the side, sparks and embers spraying out over them.

Demetrius turned away and covered his head, but the sasquatch and Augustyn were unable to avoid the embers. Both of them screamed and frantically waved their arms as flames climbed along the fur.

"I'm burning again!" Augustyn ran off, and the sasquatch followed, leaving Demetrius behind.

"No! Augustyn!"

Demetrius plodded through freezing mud to the opposite corner of the shack. He rounded it and started toward Cody and Greg who had stepped apart to allow both Augustyn and the sasquatch to flee between them. Both of them watched as Augustyn and the sasquatch ran out of the trees and across the open field, flames flickering behind them.

"He's got to stop running," Demetrius said, gasping for breath as he came up between them.

Cody cupped his hands around his mouth and shouted, "Augustyn! Stop, drop, and roll!"

"I can't tell which of them is which," Greg said.

"Augustyn is the shorter one," Demetrius said.

"Sasquatch on the left and Augustyn on the right?" Cody said.

"Right."

"Whose right?" Cody asked, giving him a tired grin.

"Augustyn!" Greg shouted, his voice echoing across the field. "Stop, drop, and roll!"

"Wow," Cody said. "You've still got the Dad Voice."

Out in the open field, the shorter figure on the right suddenly face-planted into the snow. The sasquatch continued to run, waving its burning arm wildly as it headed for a stand of trees far across the open field. A moment later,

Augustyn stuck his arm up out of the snow and gave them a thumbs-up sign.

"There he is," Cody said. "Everybody's favorite sasquatch stuntman."

"Let's go. We need to get him to a hospital," Demetrius said, setting off toward Augustyn.

"I hope he's got some good insurance," Greg said as he followed after them.

"I hope you know what you're going to say to Mom and everyone else once we get home," Cody said.

"I owe everybody an apology, I know that," Greg said. Demetrius walked a little faster to give them some space, but not before he heard Greg say, "Especially you, Cody. I am very, truly sorry to have done this to you."

Demetrius pulled the zipper higher on his coat as he stepped out of the trees and the wind across the field hit him full force. In the distance, a final flicker of flame showed where the sasquatch had run into the woods on the other side of the field, and Demetrius wondered what would become of it.

CHAPTER SIXTEEN

Cody took the lead on the long march back to the road, staying pretty much silent. His father followed right behind him, Augustyn came next, and Demmy brought up the rear. Cody kept his eyes on the tracks he and Demmy had left from what felt like a million years ago when they'd trekked out to retrieve the drone, which had been lost inside the burning shack.

He wanted, needed, to say something to his father, but all the words seemed jumbled together. He had no idea where to begin or how to keep his cool once he started. A tiny, flickering flame of jealousy burned in a corner of his heart, and Cody needed to ponder that feeling a little longer before he chewed his dad out. He supposed he was jealous his father had actually had the opportunity and mindset to find a place away from the mayhem of them all coming together for the holidays. How often had Cody dreamed of doing that himself? Just turn away from every responsibility and hide out, with time to think and breathe and rest.

But all of that had nothing whatsoever to do with the whole open marriage idea. Cody had been with a lot of women, but deep down in his heart, he was a traditionalist when it came to marriage. He wanted to find that one person he could spend the rest of his life with and settle down, with no other men or women on the side. He'd always been looking for that in the back of his mind each time he'd started dating someone, but he'd never found his perfect match.

Not until he realized his perfect match had been right beside him almost his entire life.

A flash fire of love erupted inside him and sent a flush of heat through Cody that left his heart pounding and his eyes watering as sudden insight about the depth of his feelings flooded him. He loved Demmy, of course, but Cody knew now just how deeply *in love* he was with him. Without Demmy beside him the past twenty-four years, he wouldn't be anywhere close to the man he was today. He wanted to build something incredible with Demmy. More than an intense affair, and more than a long term relationship. This was everything he had ever wanted and needed, and he had to find a way to let Demmy know how he felt.

He looked over his shoulder to where Demmy plodded along at the back of the line, eyes cast down to watch his footing. How had he gotten so lucky? He faced forward again and worked on catching his breath.

Demmy. It had always been Demmy.

"I gotta tell you," Augustyn said between panting breaths, "I'm not sure I'm cut out to be a sasquatch stuntman."

"Nonsense!" Cody's father exclaimed. His bright, optimistic tone rang out across the field and brought a smile to Cody as well as a flood of memories: his father reassuring him after he'd struck out in the beginning of his first season of fast pitch baseball; coaching him as they threw a football in the backyard; talking him or one of his brothers through late-night cram sessions for tests, nerves over asking out girls, and broken hearts after a break up.

"You stood up to a real-live sasquatch," his father continued. "Take that experience and the memory of the beast, and let it inform your performance. You will become the greatest sasquatch stuntman who ever lived."

"Wow," Augustyn said. "You know, Greg, I think you've got something there."

"No, Augustyn, you've got something there."

Cody's good feelings rose up against his anger and disappointment, the emotions battling inside him. Tears pooled in Cody's eyes, and he swiped them away as he slogged ahead. He was still angry at his father for what he did, but the memories and lifetime of love and support were helping to cool it, no matter how much Cody fanned the flames of his displeasure with envious thoughts and confusion and hurt about his parents' marriage.

The decision about their marriage was their business and no one else's, but it had affected his and Demmy's trip to Colorado. Cody couldn't help feeling pissed about that, and he was more than a little disappointed that the best couple his parents found consisted of dumbass Sergeant Mickey and his wife.

He just hoped to God that Mickey's wife was a lot hotter than her husband.

So, yeah… He had forgiven his father, but he wasn't ready to let go of his disappointment just yet.

"Dude, you should do a TED talk or something," Augustyn said.

"Well, I don't know about that. I just raised five sons, so I know a little about delivering the occasional pep talk."

"You're like a TV dad, you know?" Augustyn said. "You've got the right thing to say at the right time."

Cody couldn't help a snort.

"I would think my family may disagree with you on that score, Augustyn. Though you are very kind to say it."

More silence as they forged across the field. Had it taken him and Demmy this long to get to the drone? He looked toward the trees where the sasquatch had vanished from sight but saw no movement, and he wondered what would become of it. Then he realized he didn't really care. He was tired of monsters. Maybe they should change the company name from Critter Catchers to Monster Magnets.

A wink of light ahead caught his attention, and he squinted to focus his vision. He could see a truck slowly driving up the road near where they had parked, sunlight sparking off the windows.

"Is that the road?" Demmy asked.

"Looks that way," Cody said. "We just need to walk to the main road and then up the hill."

"I'm pretty tired," Augustyn said. "And my arm is really sore."

"We'll get you to the hospital," Cody said. "You three can wait at the bottom of the hill while I go get the car."

A short time later, they stepped onto the gravel of the single-lane trail they'd taken to get to the even more narrow track up the incline. Cody encouraged Augustyn to step out of sight behind a stand of trees to keep from scaring the crap out of passing drivers and avoid getting shot.

"We can look at his costume and try to figure out how to get the mask off," Demmy said, reaching out to give Cody's upper arm a squeeze. "You okay going up there alone?"

Cody heard the underlying concern in Demmy's question and knew he was asking if he was okay with his father instead of with simply going to get the car. He nodded and gave him a tight smile. "I'm good. Get that mask off Augustyn if you can, and we'll get him to the hospital." Cody looked at his father over Demmy's shoulder. "You should probably get checked out, too. Just to be safe."

His father held his arms out to the sides and smiled. "I'm just fine. See?"

"Well, let's have you looked at anyway, because Mom's probably going to want to kill you when she sees you." Cody gave him a pointed look with raised eyebrows and lips pressed tight before he turned away.

The sun was bright and shone directly in his face as he hiked up the inclined trail. When it leveled out, he paused to catch his breath as he looked out over the field they had just crossed. Smoke rose from the woods to his left, and he wondered if someone had called the fire department yet. He figured the shack would burn itself out. The fire wouldn't spread to the trees because of the heavy snow, but a fire professional should at least make sure.

A few minutes later, he reached the SUV and found the drone controller where he had dropped it on the other side of the road with his cell phone still attached. He was careful to stay back from the edge of the drop-off as he picked up the controller, and he disconnected his phone as he crossed the road to the SUV. He still had fifty percent of his battery left and a single bar of reception, so he called his mom and got into the SUV where he'd left the keys in the ignition.

"Where are you two?" His mother did not waste time on a greeting or any other pleasantries.

"We went out for some last minute Christmas shopping." He couldn't resist a bit of teasing.

"Oh, Cody. We've all got enough stuff. We just need your father back. Come join us. We've moved to a different search location."

"Is everyone there with you?"

"Yes, your brothers are all here. We'd really like to see you."

"I'd like to see you all, too. But you're going to have to

come to me. I have a present for all of you that I need to give you today."

"We don't need any presents. Are you not listening to me?"

"I'm listening to you, but I don't think you're listening to me. Will you listen?"

"Fine. I'm listening. What do you need to tell me?"

"I found Dad."

The silence which followed lasted so long Cody was afraid he'd lost the signal. Then she gasped, and he heard her turn away to shout, "He's found!" She was back on the phone as a chorus of cheers went up in the background, and Cody was surprised by tears flooding his eyes.

"Oh thank God! Where? Where did you find him? Where are you? Is he okay?"

"He's fine. But we met someone who is hurt, so we're taking them both to the hospital."

"Oh no. But your father is safe and okay?"

"He is. But which hospital should I take them to? I'll put the name in my GPS and meet you there."

"Well, I don't know. We would go to St. Anthony's from the house. Can you get him there?"

"I will. Meet us in the ER."

"Oh, thank God. Thank you, Cody. Drive safe. I love you."

"Love you, too. And we'll be there as soon as we can."

Cody ended the call as he turned off the snow-covered track and onto the gravel trail. Greg got into the front passenger seat and moved it up to give Augustyn leg room as Demmy got in behind Cody.

"Was your phone still there?" Demmy asked.

Cody held it up. "Still there. Where's yours?"

"Hopefully in that center console."

Cody opened the console and handed Demmy's phone back. He typed St. Anthony's into his GPS and once the directions came up, he handed his phone to his father and looked in the back to make sure everyone was settled. His eyebrows went up as he found himself looking at Augustyn's face instead of the sasquatch mask.

"Well, hi. Good to finally see your face."

Augustyn's blond hair was plastered to his skull with sweat. He had big blue eyes, a large, sloped nose, and a gap between his two front bottom teeth Cody would bet money he sprayed water through as a party trick. A long, dark blond goatee twisted into a single braid clung to his chin and trembled with each spoken word.

"Feels good to have that mask off," Augustyn said. "Thought I might have to sleep in it."

"You wearing anything under the body suit?" Cody's father asked.

"Oh yeah. A pair of all-in-one long-johns."

"I hope they're red," Cody said.

Augustyn looked confused. "Is there any other color?"

"Good man." Cody faced forward and pulled onto the road. "We're heading to St. Anthony's. Demmy, can you call 911 and report the fire?"

Demmy called and relayed the location based on the road names from Cody's GPS. When he'd disconnected, he asked Augustyn about his arm, and as they talked in the backseat, Cody glanced at his father. He gave his dad a tight smile before looking back at the road. His father touched him on the arm and leaned in a little closer.

"I'm very sorry for worrying you, son."

Cody gave him a side-eye. "I accept your apology. But it's not me you really need to apologize to."

His father looked tired and more than a little nervous as he nodded. "You're right."

"Just so you're ready."

It took forty minutes to get to St. Anthony's, and Cody pulled up to the emergency entrance where his father,

Demmy, and Augustyn all got out. Cody lowered his window as Demmy stepped up.

"We found your dad," Demmy said with a smile. "It's a Christmas Eve miracle."

"Yeah." He watched his father and Augustyn standing inside the doors talking to a security guard who appeared to be very nervous about Augustyn's costume. "That it is."

"And we got to see one of the country's greatest legends up close."

Cody gave him a sour look. "Not sure I'd line that up in the pro column."

Demmy smirked. "You doing okay?"

"I'll be fine. Just worried about my mom and brothers. Not sure how they're going to handle it once they find out Dad willfully hid from us all. And I still don't know how to process the whole open marriage thing."

"A lot of couples make that kind of arrangement work. And your dad was being stalked by a sasquatch, so he's got that to fall back on."

"Yeah. There's that." Cody let out a heavy breath then gave Demmy a long, serious look. "Just so you know, I'm not interested in an open relationship."

Demmy raised his eyebrows and smiled. "Well, that's good to hear."

"Would that be something you'd want?"

He shook his head. "Not at all."

Cody's muscles relaxed a bit as he nodded. "Good. Can you hang out with them inside while I find a parking spot?"

"I'll make sure they don't try to ship Augustyn to a veterinarian or something."

"That would be the icing on the cake, wouldn't it?"

After he found a parking space and made his way into the emergency room, Cody found Demmy on his feet leaning back against a wall. Most of the chairs in the waiting area were taken and a number of the occupants looked pale, sweaty, and ill.

"Yikes," Cody said as he surveyed the crowd. "Looks like a plague hospital."

"Yeah, this is about as close as I want to get to them." Demmy wiped his palms on his thighs. "I guess there's been an outbreak of the flu. Right now I really just want a hot shower."

"I can't imagine why. Dad and Augustyn already go back?"

Demmy nodded. "Augustyn's costume was causing some commotion out here, so they decided to take him first, and he requested your dad go with him."

"Nice those two have bonded." Cody couldn't keep the snark out of his voice.

Before Demmy could respond, a nurse approached. "Mr. Bower?"

"Yeah, that's me."

"Your father's asked for you to come back." She looked over at Demmy. "Both of you."

A bout of wet, deep coughing erupted from the waiting area, and Cody waved for the nurse to precede them. "Right behind you."

Augustyn and Cody's father were in neighboring beds with a curtain between them. Demmy stopped to watch the medical team cut away the arm of Augustyn's costume as Cody stepped into his father's area. He was hooked up to a heart monitor, and they had inserted an IV in the back of his hand.

"Hi, son." His father waved toward the heart monitor. "This is all just a precaution after I told them I'd been in a shack for a couple of nights."

"Better to be safe."

"That's what I thought as well."

A male nurse walked in at a fast clip. He shot a glance at Cody, then did a double take.

"Have you been seen yet?" the nurse asked.

Cody looked over his shoulder, thinking maybe Augustyn had wandered in, but no one was behind him. He frowned at the nurse. "Who, me?"

"You've got dried blood on the side of your neck."

Cody reached to the back of his head and winced at the sting. "Oh. I didn't realize that."

"Sit down there." The nurse pointed to a white plastic chair as he pulled on gloves. After checking Cody's father's IV and heart monitor, the nurse changed into a fresh pair of gloves. "Looks like a small cut. I don't think it will need stitches."

"That's a relief." Cody flinched away from the nurse's exploring fingers. "Ow."

Demmy stepped into view, and his eyes went wide as he saw the nurse examining the back of Cody's head. "What happened?"

The nurse looked up. "Friend of yours?"

Cody grimaced as he met Demmy's gaze. "The best."

"That's from when you got thrown into the wall," Demmy said.

"Thrown?" The nurse stepped in front of Cody and looked between the three of them. "Do I need to get a police officer in here?"

"No, it's nothing like that," Cody said. "We were looking through some old shack out in the woods, and I tripped and hit my head."

"That's really different from getting thrown into a wall." The nurse gave Demmy a pointed look. "Be careful how you phrase things in the ER."

Demmy nodded. "Understood. Sorry."

"Your friend won't need stitches, but the skin will be tender back here."

Cody winced and looked up at Demmy. "Just another trip to see the family."

"Is this why you don't come out more often?" his father asked.

At that moment, Cody's mother stepped up beside Demmy. When she saw Cody's father, her hand went to her mouth and tears filled her eyes. "Greg!"

"Hello dear," Cody's father said, his own eyes filling with tears. "Now, don't cry."

"Who's this?" the nurse asked Cody as he cleaned the wound.

"My mother." He hissed and shrank away from the sting of antiseptic. "Damn, man, give me a safe word or something." He looked at his mother. "Mom, where's everybody else?"

"I sent them on to the house," she said, voice thick with tears as she stood over his father and held his face between her palms. "It would have been a circus to have all of us back here."

"That's a sweet scene," the nurse said.

"Yeah. They've been married forty years."

"Long time." The nurse lowered his voice and asked, "How long have you and your best friend been together?"

Cody half-turned to look at him. "That obvious?"

"Not really. The ER gives me a bit more insight into people."

"Over twenty years as best friends. Just a few months as something more."

"Great way for it to go," the nurse said. "Friends first. That'll help you get through the hard times."

"What are you, some kind of psychic or something?"

"Nope. Just an attentive nurse. Name's Will, by the way."

"Cody." He gestured to where Demmy stood in the aisle, looking between Augustyn's area and the one where Cody sat with his mother and father. "That's Demmy."

"Demmy?"

"Short for Demetrius."

"Got it."

Demmy heard his name and stepped into the curtained area. "You call me?"

Cody grinned. "Not yet. Just telling Will here about you. About us."

"I'm Will. Good to meet you."

"Oh, hi. Demetrius."

"So I hear."

Demmy cocked his head and smiled quizzically at Cody. "You told him about us?"

"I guessed," Will said. "Hold still. Almost done."

"He guessed."

"Oh. We that obvious?"

"No," Will replied. "I'm just observant. Okay, the cut is cleaned out and bandaged. You should change the bandage again tonight and keep the area clean."

"Bandage?" Cody's mother came around the end of the bed. "What happened?"

"Just a minor accident," Cody said. "No big deal."

A ruckus erupted from the other side of the curtain, and a woman shouted, "Oh my God! Do you know how much that suit costs?"

"Never a dull moment," Will muttered. "Stay here." He peeled off his gloves, pumped some antibacterial gel onto his hands and hurried out.

Cody heard him talking as he walked into Augustyn's space. "I need everyone in here to leave right now except for the patient and the nurse."

"I'm the DA from his movie," the woman said. "I need to stay here."

"Sorry, I don't know what a DA is," Will said.

"Director's Assistant. Augustyn is my responsibility. He's covered under the studio's insurance, so I need to be consulted before any care is delivered."

"Perfect. Glad you're here. Let's get you talking to a doctor."

"Don't cut any more of that suit away," the woman practically shouted before Will led her down the aisle toward the nurses' station.

Cody took his mother's hand and gave it a squeeze. "Sorry we messed up Christmas Eve."

She looked surprised. "Messed it up? You made it the best Christmas Eve ever. You found your father."

Cody exchanged a grin with his father. "Yeah. I found him." He took Demmy's hand and looked up at him. "Correction: we found him. I couldn't have done it without Demmy."

Cody's mother pulled Demmy into a strong hug. "Thank you, Demetrius. I'm so glad you're a part of our family."

Demmy smiled at Cody over her shoulder as he returned her hug. "I am, too."

"Did I miss something?" Cody's father asked.

"Oh, yeah, I forgot you weren't there." Cody paused to let his words sink in before he continued. "Demmy and I are together now. We're a couple." He looked at Demmy, and they smiled at each other.

"I think that's wonderful!" his father exclaimed. "Welcome to our family, Demetrius. Although you've been part of our family as long as I can remember, now it's in an official capacity."

Augustyn stepped into view and Cody's mother shouted in surprise. He still wore his costume, and part of the burned sleeve had been cut away. Augustyn had brought the IV stand with him, and gave them all a doped-up smile. "Merry Christmas, everyone."

"Oh, good grief," Cody's mother said. "What the hell is he supposed to be?"

"That's Augustyn," Cody's father said with a chuckle. "He helped rescue me."

"Why's he dressed like that?" She backed slowly away from Augustyn.

"Why don't you sit down, Mom? And let Dad and me tell you all about it."

CHAPTER SEVENTEEN

fter Cody's father had been examined by a doctor and released, they met police sergeant Mickey Hastings as they were heading for the exit. Demetrius leaned in close to Cody and whispered, "Easy."

Demetrius found the tension and awkwardness between Sergeant Hastings, Greg, and Alice hard to watch. After a few fumbling attempts, the sergeant was able to get around to his questions about Greg's disappearance. Cody suggested they move to a more private place, and one of the nurses showed them to a vacant conference room away from the crowded ER.

Greg did most of the talking, and left out no details of the days he'd been missing. As he described hitting the sasquatch and it chasing him into the night, Demetrius watched Mickey and Alice's expressions. They both looked surprised, and then nervous. Demetrius figured that any mention of the monster would not make it into the final police report. That was probably for the best.

He let his mind drift as Greg and Cody talked, thinking about the last sight he had of the sasquatch disappearing into the trees with one arm still ablaze. Maybe the monster had finally extinguished the flames itself in some water or the snow, or had even tripped and put the flames out. Perhaps the fire had burned just the hair and left the skin mostly untouched. Or it could have run until the flames had become too much and then collapsed and died. Maybe some hunter or hiker would stumble across the body in the near future and the media would have a field day with the discovery.

Until that day, however, the report Sergeant Mickey Hastings would file would most likely contain no mention of sasquatch.

Augustyn wandered past the open conference room door, then returned and stood looking in at them with a smile. He had removed the rest of his sasquatch costume and the red all-in-ones and now wore a pair of scrubs that only extended down to his calves. His arm was heavily bandaged and his eyes glassy with painkillers.

"Dudes, there you are. That was one wild ride." Augustyn entered the room and bro-hugged Greg, Cody, and then Demetrius. He flashed a drugged smile at the sergeant, seeming to consider whether or not he should bro-hug him before deciding against it and pulling Alice into a bear hug.

"Thank you for helping bring my husband back to us," Alice said, her voice muffled against Augustyn's chest.

"My pleasure." Augustyn flashed his dazed smile once more before wandering off.

"Augustyn!"

The close-to-breaking tone belonged to the director's assistant of *Killer 'Squatch!* She hurried past the door after Augustyn, and moments later went by in the opposite direction, leading him by his uninjured arm. Mickey called out and handed her a card, telling her to call the station when Augustyn was in a better frame of mind to give a statement.

"That would have been about six years ago," she said, "before he became a pot-head."

"How about when he's just a little more lucid?" Mickey said.

"Fine." She gave Augustyn's arm a gentle tug and led him away.

The sun was going down as they left the hospital and climbed into Alice's SUV, Cody behind the wheel and Demetrius sitting in the front passenger seat. Greg and Alice held hands in the backseat as Cody drove back to the house. The moment they came to a stop in the driveway, the entire family rushed the car. Shouting and laughter echoed through the night as the group of them headed back inside.

While they'd been away, Cody's brothers and their families had all been busy preparing Christmas Eve dinner. The smell of the food made Demetrius's stomach growl, and he realized he hadn't eaten anything since the bowl of cereal he'd had for breakfast.

As the family talked and laughed, Cody caught Demetrius's eye and tipped his head toward the back door. Demetrius headed that direction as Cody whispered something to his mother, and she nodded. Cody joined Demetrius, and they slipped outside, leaving the ruckus of his family behind.

The air was cold and the night sky clear. There was no wind, no car or truck going past, no animal sounds. Everything was covered in snow and completely still. They stood on the small back porch looking at the brilliant stars, then they looked at each other.

"Your family really knows how to do Christmas Eve."

"Never a dull moment. Dinner's going to be a little while yet. Let's go get cleaned up."

After Cody had finished his shower, Demetrius checked the cut on the back of his head. Everything looked good, and he put on a fresh bandage then placed a gentle kiss on Cody's shoulder before getting in the shower himself. As if by unspoken agreement, neither pursued anything more. The day had taken too much out of them to consider sex.

Dinner was a noisy event. The food was delicious and the conversation chaotic. All hard feelings and confrontations had been put aside for the time being, and everyone was all smiles and laughter. Demetrius was especially glad to see Cody smiling and laughing, apparently having let go of his anger and confusion with his parents. Once everyone had eaten their fill, Greg stood up and surveyed them, smiling as tears shone in his eyes. The group quieted and looked at him.

"You okay, Dad?" Cody asked.

"Oh, I'm fine, just fine." Greg paused to clear his throat before he raised his glass of wine. "I want to toast all of you. I haven't always been a good father or grandfather." He looked at Alice. "Or husband. I've been callous and aloof, and at times probably downright mean. I acted in a very selfish manner this week, and I want to ask for your forgiveness."

"Selfish?" Roman shook his head. "Dad, you ran off the road and got lost out in the woods."

Demetrius exchanged a look with Cody.

"That's not what we told you, Roman," Greg said.

Roman rolled his eyes. "I know it's not what you told me, but it's what makes the most sense."

"Did you just call Dad a liar, Romes?" Grant asked.

"No," Roman snapped. "I just think he got confused while he was out in the elements for so long."

"Did you tell a fib, Grandpa?" Dexter asked in a quiet voice. "Santa won't come if you told a fib."

Grant turned to his son and said, "Grandpa didn't tell a lie, big Dex. It's just a long, confusing story. Remember how we tried to read *The Lord of the Rings* last year and it was too long and had too many names for you to follow?"

Dexter wrinkled his nose and nodded.

"Sometimes life can be like *The Lord of the Rings*."

"Long and confusing?" Dexter asked.

"That's for sure," Dave muttered, and everyone chuckled.

"Anyway," Greg said. "Whatever you choose to believe, just know this family means more to me than anything. I love you all more than you could possibly know, and I would be nothing without each of you. I wouldn't exchange any of you for someone else."

Greg looked right at Alice as he made the final statement, and Demetrius had to resist looking over at Cody. This was, by far, the most unusual Christmas Eve he'd ever experienced.

"So, let's clear the dishes and let dinner settle a bit, shall we?" Greg said, holding his glass high. "Merry Christmas."

Everyone toasted him. "Merry Christmas."

The entire group helped clear the table and pack the leftover food away. A pot of coffee was started and the dishwasher loaded. Once all of that was done, everyone gathered in the living room around the large Christmas tree with piles of beautifully wrapped gifts beneath.

"Do we get to open one present tonight?" Brock's eyes were wide, and he danced from foot to foot.

"Of course!" Alice said. "But just one."

The kids shouted with excitement, even Grant's oldest son, Conrad. There was a flurry of activity around the tree as each kid inspected their gifts, weighing them and measuring one against the other. Alice waded into the fray, laughing and teasing her grandchildren, then handed a number of gifts out to Greg. She escaped from the chaos around the tree and helped Greg distribute gifts to each of the Bower men and their significant others.

Alice approached Demetrius and leaned down close to look him in the eye.

"Santa came early for you," she said, her voice quiet and a small smile making her eyes twinkle.

"Oh?" Demetrius accepted an envelope she held out to him. "Thank you."

"What's that?" Cody leaned closer on the love seat. "Mom gave you a gift? I didn't get anything."

"It's for the both of you," Alice said. "I just thought Demetrius would appreciate it more."

Demetrius opened the envelope and pulled out a Christmas card. He smiled at the picture on the front: a snow-covered cannabis plant with a bright red cardinal wearing a rasta cap perched on one of the branches. Cody grunted and looked up at his mother. "Cute, Mom."

She tried to look innocent. "What?"

When Demetrius opened the card, two joints and a business card fell into his lap. He instinctively put a hand over the joints to hide them from the kids, then realized there was a marijuana greenhouse just outside and laughed at himself. The printed message inside the card read "Wishing you good times and good cheer during the holidays. And lots of baked goods." He laughed, and then picked up the joints and the business card.

"What's that?" Cody asked.

Demetrius handed him the joints. "I would assume a couple of free samples."

"They're both High Altitude," Greg said with a smile. "It's got a nice side effect."

Demetrius exchanged a grin with Cody. Too bad they were sleeping on Grant's living room floor and wouldn't have a chance to indulge.

"I know what these are," Cody said as he accepted the joints. "What's the business card?"

"It's to a hotel," Demetrius said, giving Alice and Greg a puzzled look. "What's this?"

"You have a room reserved starting tomorrow evening," Greg said.

"What?" Cody looked at the card and back at his parents. "You kicking us out?"

"Our gift to you both this year is a room at the Rocky Peak Hotel, down the road," Alice said.

"What?" Roman said from across the room. "They get a hotel room?"

"They do indeed," Alice said.

"That's not fair!" Roman was practically whining.

"Roman Jovi Bower, you stop that whining right now," Alice said.

"Uh oh, Romes," Grant said with a grin, "Mom used your full name. You're in trouble now."

"You want to start with me too, Grant Halen Bower?" Alice pinned him down with an icy stare.

"Ooo," Cody's other two brothers said.

"David Floyd and Brady Mercury, do you have anything to add?" Alice put her hands on her hips as she looked from one of her sons to the other.

"No, ma'am," they all said at the same time, and the five kids and four significant others all giggled.

"Oh my God," Brady's wife, Hilari said. "You all have middle names from 80's musicians?"

Demetrius was just as surprised as Hilari, and glad she had asked the question. He had been planning to ask Cody about it later when they were alone.

"I happened to love that music," Alice said, hands still on her hips. "I still do, as a matter of fact."

"It's true," Greg said. "She rarely changes the car radio off that Sirius 80s station."

"These boys should be proud of the history of their given middle names," Alice said.

"I don't know if 'proud' is really how I'd label what I'm feeling right now," Dave grumbled.

"Alice and Greg, this is a very kind gift," Demetrius said. "But how did you get a room on Christmas Day? I can't imagine they would have anything available."

"We know the owner," Greg said with a shrug. "He always keeps a room or two free for last minute emergencies."

"Well, thank you very much," Demetrius said, smiling at Cody. "That's really nice, isn't it?"

"Yeah, it's a great gift," Cody said. "We really appreciate it."

"You can check in tomorrow early afternoon," Alice said. "And you have it for two nights. It's on the way for us to come pick you up to take you to the airport when you leave on the twenty-seventh."

Demetrius got up and hugged them in turn. "Thank you so much. This is a really wonderful gift."

"You brought Greg home," Alice said. "And it's not fair for you to sleep on Grant's floor. You need a holiday, too."

"I'm glad we found him," Demetrius said.

"Yeah, no matter how weird of a situation it was," Cody added, fixing his father with a look. "Both before and after."

"We're not a perfect couple," Greg said, and put his arm around Alice's shoulders. "But we're in it to the end."

"Which won't be for a while yet," Alice said. She put a hand on Greg's chest and smiled up at him.

"And you guys are okay now?" Cody asked in a low voice.

Greg looked down at Alice, his expression so serious and intense, it momentarily stopped Demetrius's breath.

"We're getting better," Greg said.

"We know what we need to work on," Alice added. "And we're committed to working on it."

Dexter ran up behind Alice and wrapped his arms around her waist from behind. "Grandma! I love it!"

"Oh my goodness, let me see which present you opened," Alice said, Dexter leading her back toward the Christmas tree.

Cody took a step closer to his father and put a hand on his shoulder. "You sure you're going to be okay, Dad?"

Greg smiled and nodded. "Your mother and I will be just fine, son. Don't worry. I won't go running off again, I promise."

Cody nodded, then gestured to the Christmas card Demetrius still held. "You didn't have to do that, you know."

"I know. But we wanted to. You both deserve to have some peace and quiet for the last couple of nights you're here. It's your holiday, too."

"Well, thank you," Cody said. "And our backs thank you even more."

They laughed and when they turned to check out the gifts everyone else received, Demetrius's phone buzzed in his pocket.

"It's Amelia," he said to Cody after checking. "I'll be right back."

"Wish her a Merry Christmas from me."

"I will."

Demetrius accepted the call as he stepped into the kitchen.

"Merry Christmas, Aunt Amelia."

"Merry Christmas, Demetrius. How are things going out there?"

"Oh, you know, the usual." Demetrius glanced over his shoulder to make sure no one had followed him into the kitchen and lowered his voice a little. "Got chased through the snow by an urban legend as we were searching for Cody's dad who had been missing since the day we arrived."

"What?"

Amelia's shriek forced Demetrius to pull the phone away from his ear. When he carefully brought it back, he could hear her talking fast and had to really focus to follow what she was saying.

"Another monster case? How many is that now? What kind of monster was it? Is Cody's father okay? Are you and Cody okay? Did you get any proof?"

"Whoa, whoa, whoa," Demetrius said with a quiet laugh. "Slow down, Aunt Amelia. Slow down."

"Well you can't drop a bomb like that and expect me not to react." She took a breath and let it out. "Okay, tell me everything. But first, are you and Cody okay? You're not hurt?"

"Not hurt. Well, not bad. Cody has a bandage on the back of his head, and there was a fire, but we didn't get burned."

"Bandage? Fire? Oh my God, is he all right?"

"He's doing well. He's in with his family right now. They're all opening one gift for Christmas Eve."

"Oh, do you need to go?"

"No. I already opened my gift. It's a hotel room for Cody and me for the next two nights."

"Oh, that sounds nice. Now, tell me about this monster. What was it?"

"It was everyone's favorite classic, a sasquatch."

Amelia let out another shriek. "Oh, Christmas trees, I missed it! He's always been my favorite. Figures I would get stuck with a swamp monster."

Demetrius laughed, and it felt so good he laughed some more. Amelia joined in, and they laughed together for several minutes. Cody poked his head through the doorway and grinned.

"What's so funny?" he asked. "Did Otis give Amelia something dirty for Christmas?"

Demetrius shook his head as he caught his breath. "No! Stop that. Amelia's upset we ran into sasquatch without her. He's her favorite."

"Tell her she got a swamp monster."

"She is very disappointed with the monster she got stuck with."

Cody's father called to him from the living room, saying they all wanted to talk with Grandma Felicia. Cody stared at Demetrius with wide eyes for a moment, then whispered, "Help me," before he staggered out of the kitchen.

"Okay, now tell me everything," Amelia said. "And don't leave out any details."

Demetrius grinned. "It started the night we arrived…"

CHAPTER EIGHTEEN

Cody wheeled his large suitcase into the hotel lobby, Demmy right behind him. Instrumental versions of Christmas carols played through hidden speakers, and the tantalizing smell of fresh coffee wafted over from a sideboard. The lobby was clean and calm, and not one member of his family was anywhere in sight. He felt a bit more tension leave him, and he lowered his shoulders and let out a long breath.

He couldn't wait to sleep in a big, soft hotel bed instead of in a sleeping bag on Grant's living room floor. He would pull Demmy in close, and no one would wake them late at night by turning on a kitchen light or creeping around searching for a misplaced book or phone.

And there would be no monsters. No monsters at all.

"Wow, this is nice," Demmy said as he looked around the spacious, well-appointed lobby. "Your parents really went all out for us."

"Let's hold off on that statement until we see the room," Cody said.

"Hello gentlemen," a pretty young girl called from behind

the check-in desk. "Merry Christmas, and welcome to the Rocky Peak Hotel. May I help you with something?"

"Yeah, hi." Cody left his bag with Demmy and crossed to the desk. "Merry Christmas to you as well. We should have a reservation for Cody Bower and Demetrius Singleton."

The girl's fingers flew over her keyboard, and she smiled at her computer screen. She looked up at Cody, glanced over at Demmy, then looked back at the screen as she typed a bit.

"Everything okay?" Cody asked.

She nodded. "Everything is just..." She hit a key and nodded at the screen before looking at him. "Perfect. I've upgraded your room to the Sunrise Suite. It's one of our nicest rooms, and since you're a special guest, and it's Christmas Day, it seems like a good fit."

"No virgin birth for us tonight then, huh?" Cody said with a smirk.

"Pardon?" The girl cocked her head as she flashed a tentative smile.

"You've upgraded us to a suite, so apparently there's plenty of room at this inn." He shook his head. "Forget it, bad joke. Sorry, it's been a long week."

Her smile brightened. "I got the joke. I was just teasing you." She handed him two keycards and pointed toward the elevators. "You're on the tenth floor, room 1050. When you get off the elevator, make a left and go all the way to the end of the hall. It's a corner suite, facing east. I think you'll really like the room. Call down to the desk if you need anything brought up to you."

"Thank you," Cody said. "For the upgrade, and for not making me feel too stupid about my bad joke."

"Enjoy your stay."

"Making friends?" Demmy asked once Cody returned to where he waited.

"I'm a friendly guy."

"That you are. Come on, I'm ready for a shower and a long winter's nap."

"You didn't sleep well our final night on Grant's floor?" Cody pulled his suitcase toward the elevators.

"I woke up to find Mac moving silently around us like some kind of bald Jedi creeper."

"When was this?"

"About three in the morning."

"I didn't wake up?"

"You were snoring and slept through it all." Demmy yawned as they got on the elevator.

"I was snoring?"

"You were snoring."

Cody made a face. "Was I loud?"

"You weren't as loud as when you come."

Cody laughed, then blushed and pulled Demmy close for a tight hug.

"You never cease to surprise me," Cody said. "I love you."

"I love you, too."

The elevator doors opened on the tenth floor, and Cody led the way down the hall to the door with a plaque that read Sunrise Suite.

"The Sunrise Suite?" Demmy looked impressed. "We're really that important?"

"I may have charmed my way into an upgrade." Cody slid the key into the lock and a green light flashed.

"Was it you being charming, or your parents paying an extra fee?"

"To-may-to, to-mah-to."

Cody stepped into the room and took in their lodgings. The door opened into a short entry way with a mirrored closet on one side and a door leading to a full bathroom on the other. Beyond the entry was a sitting room with a sofa and two chairs in front of a gas fireplace with a TV hung on the wall above it. A small kitchen behind a tall dine-in counter was just to their left and French doors on their right led to a large bedroom. Directly across from the entry was a sliding glass door that opened onto a balcony with a view of the mountains.

"Wow," Demmy said. "This is amazing."

"We must have been really good this year," Cody said.

"I guess tracking down your dad and fighting off an angry sasquatch go a long ways."

Cody hung his head and put his hands on his hips. "A fucking sasquatch. Can you believe it?"

Demmy grinned and shrugged one shoulder. "Yeah. I mean, it's us, you know?"

"Yeah. But is one trip without a monster too much to ask?"

"Let's plan another trip and see what happens."

"I'll think about it."

They entered the bedroom, both sighing as they laid side-by-side across the king-sized bed.

"This mattress is amazing," Cody said.

"I think I just fell asleep," Demmy said, eyes closed and hands folded across his chest.

Cody pushed up on one elbow and leaned over to kiss him softly. "Don't fall asleep yet. I have plans for you."

Demmy opened one eye. "That sounds promising."

Cody got up and searched through his suitcase until he found the two joints his parents had given them. He held them up and waggled his eyebrows. "Feel like sharing a joint?"

Demmy sat up and grinned. "It feels like we're being really bad, even though it's totally legal out here."

"That's the best part."

"I just want to shower first, okay?" Demmy said.

"Yeah, me too. You can go first."

Cody found robes and slippers in the bedroom closet and

went about unpacking some clothes until Demmy had finished his shower. Once they had both showered, they wore just the robes and slippers and stepped out on the small balcony with a joint. The wind had calmed, and the sun was out, melting the snow off the sidewalks and streets. Cody lit up, took the first hit, then handed it to Demmy.

"It's not too cold," Demmy said as he accepted the joint. "Just a bit of an updraft that makes me feel bad for women when they wear skirts in the winter."

They smoked and talked about Cody's family as they looked out at the mountains in the distance. It felt good to just stand there together with nowhere to rush off to and no one moving around in the background. Once they had finished the joint, Cody smiled and leaned in for a soft, sweet kiss.

"Let's go inside," he said.

They stood at the foot of the bed and kissed for a time, not in a rush to go any faster or get naked. Cody's mind was calm and quiet, and he lost himself in a long kissing session. After several minutes, Demmy finally opened his robe and gently untied the belt on Cody's. Still kissing, Cody pulled him close and they both moaned as their erections pressed together. Cody slid his hands inside Demmy's robe and around to his bare back.

"I really like this stuff," Demmy said.

Cody leaned back and grinned. "My stuff?"

"Well, yeah, of course. But I was talking about the joint. Who would have ever suspected that your brother would develop an aphrodisiac. What do you call the different variety of marijuana? Is it a flavor? A strain? A type?"

"I don't know, and I don't care. I just like what it does."

Cody kissed him again, then leaned lower to kiss and suck each nipple. He stooped over to place a kiss in the center of his torso and then got on his knees, reaching up to flick his thumbs over Demmy's nipples. Keeping up steady movements with his thumbs, Cody took Demmy's cock in his mouth and slowly sucked him.

"Oh, Cody," Demmy said.

Pulling back, Cody regarded Demmy's length as he stroked it. His conversation with Dave about being with men had been running on a loop in the back of his mind ever since that evening. For a while now, Cody had been thinking about changing things up a bit when it came to sex with Demmy, and with the effects of the weed, the moment seemed more than perfect. He didn't want to hesitate or second guess himself; he just wanted to act.

"Don't lose that thought," Cody said and got to his feet. He yanked the bed covers back, sending a few of the pillows flying across the room.

Demmy laughed and let the robe fall off his shoulders as he stepped out of the slippers. "You are really excited about having our own room."

"Fuck yeah, I am. Aren't you?"

Demmy grabbed his hand and pulled him close for a deep, tongue-heavy kiss. "Abso-fuckin-lutely."

"What you do to me," Cody whispered and quickly kissed him again. "Lie down."

"Ass up or down?" Demmy asked as he crawled onto the bed.

"On your back."

Cody grabbed the bottle of lube from his toiletries kit and walked across the bed on his knees. After another kiss, he moved down to lick and suck each nipple, then moved lower still to dip the tip of his tongue into Demmy's navel. He slowly painted a line of saliva down to Demmy's cock and took him into his mouth.

"Come up here. I want to suck you, too."

Cody laid down and shifted into position. Demmy rolled

onto his side, and they sucked each other. As he worked his mouth along Demmy's dick, Cody fondled his balls and slid a finger back to circle Demmy's anus. He lifted his top knee to allow Demmy room to move, and he copied the same moves on Cody.

Cody shifted position again so he was face-to-face with Demmy. He kissed him and flipped open the lube to squirt a generous amount onto Demmy's fingers.

"I like where this is going," Demmy said, reaching down to his own ass.

"No. I want you to lube me up," Cody said.

"Oh, okay." Demmy took hold of his cock, but Cody shook his head.

"No. My ass."

"Need a finger up there?"

"Your dick."

Demmy's eyes widened. "Are you sure?"

Cody nodded, heart pounding. "I'm nervous, but really fucking turned on. It's partly the pot, but mostly it's you."

Demmy beamed. "You're really sure?"

"I am. Just… go slow and use a lot of lube."

"Oh, I will. But first, I'm going to eat your ass like a Christmas ham."

Demmy pushed Cody onto his back and lifted his legs to get at his ass. He ran his tongue up the crack of Cody's ass and over the ridges of his anus.

"Oh, fuck, I love when you rim me."

"So do I."

Demmy propped him up with his hands on both ass cheeks and spread him open. Cody moaned as Demmy licked, sucked, and drilled his tongue into his anus. When Cody's hole was wet with spit, Demmy eased a finger inside, watching his face the whole time.

"Feel okay?" Demmy asked.

Cody nodded. "Yeah. Feels good. You've fingered me before, but today I want your dick."

"Oh man, you have no idea how fucking hard I am right now."

"Me, too."

Demmy licked Cody's taint and balls as he finger-fucked him. He added lube and a second finger, continuing to lick and suck his balls as he slowly stroked Cody's dick with his free hand.

"Think you're ready?" Demmy asked.

Cody nodded. His chest felt hot and tight, and his muscles trembled. He was nervous, but he wanted this. He needed to have Demmy inside him.

"It might be easier to start if you get on top," Demmy said. "I know it was for me my first time."

"Yeah? Okay. I can do that."

Demmy stretched out on his back, and Cody sat astride his thighs. He squeezed a generous amount of lube into his palm and slicked up Demmy's cock. It was hard and hot in his grip, and he licked his lips as he thought about the broad head spreading his sphincter and sliding inside.

"As slow as you need to take it," Demmy said, then gasped and squirmed. "Ease up on the stroking or you're going to make me come too soon."

Cody leaned down for a gentle, loving kiss, then got on his feet. He squatted and reached back to guide Demmy's cock. The slick head poked him just beneath his anus, and he aimed it higher. It pressed at the center of his hole, and he closed his eyes and supported himself on the mattress with his free hand. With slow, steady movements, Cody lowered himself onto Demmy. He winced at the initial entry, rising up a bit to try from another angle.

"God, your ass feels so fucking good."

"Did your dick get twice as big in the last minute?"

"I told you it was really fucking hard. If you need to stop, that's okay."

"Fuck, no." Cody put both hands on Demmy's chest and slowly, steadily sat on him. When the entry began to burn, he rose up and started again. Soon he was moving faster, taking Demmy's dick a little deeper with each pass. "I'm glad I've increased my squat reps at the gym."

Demmy moaned and nodded. "Not as glad as I am. Fuck, your ass is so hot."

After a bit of time, Cody finally sat on Demmy's hips, fully impaled. He tipped his head back and closed his eyes, pausing to let his body adjust to their fit. The initial feeling of fullness had passed, replaced by pressure on his prostate that sent tingles through his groin.

"Okay, you're in," Cody said, and he leaned down for another kiss. "And now I want you on top. My legs are shot."

"Whatever you want."

Cody eased off Demmy and laid on his back. He took a moment to stretch his legs, kneading the tight muscles. When they felt ready, he raised his legs and grabbed the backs of his knees, exposing himself. Demmy walked up the mattress on his knees, slowly stroking lube along his length as he approached.

"You look so hot right now," Demmy said. "It feels like this is all a dream or something."

"This whole trip has felt like a dream," Cody said. "This is just the good part of it."

Demmy let Cody's legs rest on his shoulders and he kissed one ankle, then the other as he used a finger to apply more lube to Cody's hole. Aligning himself, Demmy eased inside, pushing steadily and pulling back to start again until he was fully seated. Staying deep inside him, Demmy stretched out over Cody's torso and kissed him.

"You're amazing," Demmy whispered.

"I feel pretty amazing right now," Cody whispered back, "thanks for noticing."

They laughed together before Demmy straightened up and started to move his hips. He was slow at first but quickly picked up the pace until he was fucking Cody fast and deep.

"Oh, fuck yeah," Cody said as he grabbed the sheet beneath him in both hands and gripped it tight. "God, fuck my ass."

"I'm close," Demmy said with a gasp. "I'm really close."

"Inside me. Come inside me."

Cody stroked himself in time with Demmy's thrusts, and just as Demmy grunted in that familiar way Cody had come to love, Cody's own orgasm rushed through him. He shouted something unintelligible as he shot across his torso, muscles clenching tight around Demmy still buried within him.

They panted as they caught their breath, then Demmy slowly pulled out, and Cody winced at the sting of his withdrawal. He dropped his legs and lay on his back staring up at the ceiling as Demmy stretched out on his side next to him and placed a hand in the center of his chest.

"That was awesome."

Cody turned his head and smiled. "Yeah it was."

They kissed, and then Demmy collapsed onto his back, and they lay side-by-side looking up at the ceiling.

"How do you feel?" Demmy finally asked.

"I feel great." Cody looked at him. "And hungry."

"That's not a surprise."

"How about we order room service? I don't want to leave the room."

"I like the sound of that. But first, I'm going to rinse off in the shower."

"That's a really good idea. Glad I thought of it."

Cody got out of bed and strode toward the bathroom. He wasn't at all surprised when a pillow hit him in the back of the head. Demmy chased him into the bathroom, and they got into the glass-walled walk-in shower. They lathered each other and took turns rinsing off under the spray. When they'd finished, they pulled on the robes and stepped into the slippers.

"I could get used to living like this," Cody said as he looked out the sliding glass door at the mountains.

"Maybe business will pick up next year, and we'll be able to afford a high-rise condominium. Sadly, the mountains back home are nowhere near the size of these."

Cody looked over his shoulder at Demmy sitting in the comfortable armchair reviewing the room service menu. The early afternoon sunlight lit him perfectly, and his thinning dark hair was tousled because he had toweled it dry and forgotten to run a comb through it. A warm feeling swelled within Cody's chest and spread quickly, making him feel a little dizzy. He turned away before Demmy could look up and see his expression which he was sure was something like shock.

Everything between them was pretty much amazing. How could Cody want anything more? Where would he ever find a relationship as fulfilling and loving as this one?

"What are you getting?" Demmy asked.

"What?"

"From the menu. Any idea what you're going to order?"

Cody walked around behind Demmy's chair and leaned in to look at the menu over his shoulder.

"Surf and turf sounds pretty damn good right now."

"You are spoiling yourself!"

"It's Christmas Day, gotta be nice to yourself this time of year."

"Sounds good to me. I'll join you."

Cody placed the order and after he hung up the phone,

tightened the belt of his robe. "Is it weird that I want to wear the robe and slippers while we eat?"

"Not at all."

"Good." Cody pulled Demmy close and kissed him. "Merry Christmas, Dems."

Demmy chuckled. "Merry Christmas, Codes."

CHAPTER NINETEEN

Demetrius climbed the final few steps, put his hands on his hips as he let out his breath, and looked at the view. "It's beautiful."

Cody came up beside him. "Oh, wow."

They stood at the top of Red Rocks Amphitheater, looking down on the bleacher-style seats that descended to the stage. It was all built right into the natural rock formations, with a wall of rock just behind the stage, and beyond that, the land sloped downward and out. The cloudless sky looked like blue neon and the snow-covered peaks of the distant mountains gleamed beneath the morning sun.

"Can you imagine seeing a concert up here?" Demetrius smiled as he looked at the beautiful view. "I don't think I'd be able to focus on the music."

"Yeah."

Demetrius looked at Cody. "You feeling all right?"

Cody darted his gaze away as he shrugged. "Yeah, I'm fine. Why?"

"You've been quiet all morning. One word answers, short sentences. Really not like you."

"You saying I talk too much?"

"Nope. Just saying that today you're not talking as much as you usually do."

Cody looked at the view again. "With something like this to look at, words don't really mean a lot, do they?"

"I guess not. Still, you were pretty talkative yesterday after we ate room service." He lowered his voice although no one else was in sight. "And you were really verbal when you fucked my ass after dinner last night."

That earned Demetrius a grin. "Yesterday was a really hot day." He turned to face Demetrius. "It's one I'll always remember."

"Yeah, me too. Your ass felt so good around my cock."

"Not just that. I'll always remember it because it made me realize that in spite of the crazy shit that happened during this trip, the fact that we were together made it all okay."

The sincerity in Cody's voice sent tingles zipping through him. Demetrius's power of speech seemed to evaporate, so he simply looked at him, taking in every detail. The bright sun brought out henna highlights in Cody's brown hair and made his brown eyes glow. He hadn't shaved in two days, and the dark scruff of beard accentuated his cheekbones and square jaw. After all the years they had been friends, Demetrius still found himself occasionally dumb-struck by Cody's attractiveness. And now that they were in a romantic relationship, he sometimes had to fight back a sense of disbelief that Cody wanted to be with him.

Cody looked toward the stage and the view beyond, then back at Demetrius. He took Demetrius's hands and smiled, and Demetrius smiled back.

"I guess what I'm trying to say is we're good together," Cody said. "Do you agree?"

Demetrius nodded. It felt like Cody was amping himself up for something, and it made Demetrius both nervous and excited. When he got nervous or excited he tended to talk too much and usually spoiled the mood, so he kept his mouth shut and let the silence stretch out until Cody continued.

"We're not just good together; we're *really* good together. And we've got a house now, thanks to Amelia. And a business, thanks to you. Everything's really good right now. But it's not perfect."

Demetrius frowned as worry suddenly twisted through his excitement. Not perfect? Had he done something wrong? Had Cody bottoming last night been too much for him in the light of morning?

Cody got down on one knee, keeping hold of both of Demetrius's hands. He looked up and smiled, so relaxed and peaceful and handsome. "Demetrius Barnaby Singleton, will you marry me?"

Everything stopped. Time, space, his thoughts, his breath… everything. Demetrius stared at Cody as his brain tried to process what had just happened.

Cody had proposed.

Cody had proposed?

Holy shit, Cody had proposed!

And Demetrius hadn't answered him yet.

"Yes!" Demetrius practically shouted, and they both laughed as he repeated it, louder each time. "Yes! Yes!! YES!!!"

Cody stood, grabbed him, and kissed him hard, tongue filling Demetrius's mouth as he pulled him tight against his body.

"I love you, Demmy," Cody whispered in his ear. "I'm so fucking in love with you, it boggles my mind."

"Me too," Demetrius whispered back. "Oh, God, me too."

They kissed again, and then Cody held him close, and they looked at the view.

"I don't have a ring," Cody said. "Sorry. This was kind of last minute."

Demetrius chuckled and squeezed him. "It's all right. I don't need a ring. Well, not yet." He squeezed again. "This has been the best Christmas ever."

"God bless us, every one."

They laughed and kissed and Demetrius couldn't wait to get back to the hotel room and celebrate.

THE END

HORROR AT HIDEAWAY COVE

CRITTER CATCHERS BOOK SIX

Demetrius and Cody return for an all new adventure in HORROR AT HIDEAWAY COVE: Critter Catchers Book Six, available now!

HORROR AT HIDEAWAY COVE

A wedding on a budget. A honeymoon booked last minute. An urban legend that rises to the surface.

After dealing with a sneaky otter and an expanding guest list, Cody and Demetrius manage to get married without a single monster crashing the event. Afterwards, Cody whisks Demmy away on the honeymoon trip he planned all on his own... after putting it off until the last minute and booking it all online, sight unseen.

To their happy surprise, the cabin Cody reserved is quite comfortable and very secluded, situated on an island in the middle of the deep Heaversford Lake, and accessible only by boat. But as usually happens to the guys, trouble has a way of finding them. For not only is the lake home to Esther, a monster similar to the one in Loch Ness, but shortly after they arrive a storm knocks out the power and a local resident drowns under mysterious circumstances. The clues all point to Esther being somehow involved, and Demetrius and Cody quickly realize they're going to have to get involved and do their own style of investigation.

Before they realize it, their peaceful honeymoon is shattered and they find themselves fighting for their lives in the cold, dark waters of Heaversford Lake.

Horror at Hideaway Cove is available in digital, print, and audio from these retailers: https://books2read.com/crittercatchers6

ABOUT THE AUTHOR

Hank Edwards (he/him) has been writing gay fiction for more than twenty years. He has published over forty novels and novellas and dozens of short stories. His writing crosses many sub-genres, including contemporary romance, rom-com, paranormal, suspense, mystery, wacky comedy, and erotica. He has written a number of series such as the funny and spooky Critter Catchers, Old West historical horror of Venom Valley, suspenseful FBI and civilian Up to Trouble, and the erotic and funny Fluffers, Inc. Under the pen name R. G. Thomas, he has written a young adult urban fantasy gay romance series called The Town of Superstition. He was born and still lives in a northwest suburb of the Motor City, Detroit, Michigan.

For more information:
www.hankedwardsbooks.com
hankedwardsbooks@gmail.com
www.facebook.com/groups/hankshangout

ALSO BY HANK EDWARDS

<u>Critter Catchers Series</u>

Terror by Moonlight

Chasing the Chupacabra

Swamped by Fear

The Devil of Pinesville

Screams of the Season

Horror at Hideaway Cove

Dread of Night

Critter Catchers Box Set 1

Critter Catchers Box Set 2

<u>Critter Catchers Universe Stories</u>

The Mystery of the Morelock Motel

<u>Critter Catchers: Level Up Series</u>

Grave Danger

Wet Screams

<u>Williamsville Inn Gay Romance:</u>

Snowflakes and Song Lyrics

The Cupid Crawl

Fake Date Flip-Flop

Star-Spangled Showdown

<u>Lacetown Murder Mysteries</u>

(co-written with Deanna Wadsworth)

Murder Most Lovely

Murder Most Deserving

Venom Valley Series

Cowboys & Vampires

Stakes & Spurs

Blood & Stone

Up to Trouble Series

Holed Up

Shacked Up

Roughed Up

Choked Up

Fluffers, Inc. Series

Fluffers, Inc.

A Carnal Cruise

Vancouver Nights

Standalone Gay Romance

Buried Secrets

Destiny's Bastard

Hired Muscle

Plus Ones

Repossession is 9/10ths of the Law

Wicked Reflection

Holiday Gay Romance:

A Gift for Greg (A Story Orgy Single)

Mistletoe at Midnight (A Story Orgy Single)

The Christmas Accomplice

Story Orgy Singles Gay Romance:

A Gift for Greg

By the Book

Cross Country Foreplay

Mistletoe at Midnight

The Cheapskate: Bad Boyfriends

With This Ring

The Story Orgy Singles Boxed Set

The Town of Superstition (YA urban fantasy series)
Published under pen name R. G. Thomas

The Midnight Gardener

The Well of Tears

The Battle of Iron Gulch

A Tangle of Secrets

Gay Erotic Short Story Collections:

A Very Dirty Dozen

Another Very Dirty Dozen

A Third Very Dirty Dozen

A Fourth Very Dirty Dozen

Salacious Singles Gay Erotic Short Stories:

Bear Market

Convoy

Double Down

Exchange Rate

Finding North

Hotel Dick

Kindred Spirits

Sacked

Stroking Midnight

Vanity Loves Company

Wet Lands